THE UNKNOWN WIFE

Mary Brendan

MILLS & BOON®

First published in Great Britain 2003
Large Print edition 2004
Harlequin Mills & Boon Limited,
Eton House, 18-24 Paradise Road, Richmond, Surrey TW9 1SR

© Mary Brendan 2003

ISBN 0 263 18187 1

Set in Times Roman 16½ on 18 pt.
42-0504-64539

Printed and bound in Great Britain
by Antony Rowe Ltd, Chippenham, Wiltshire

'I'll provide for the boy...and you too...but in my own way and on my own terms.'

'Then we have resolved nothing here this morning, Colonel Hauke. I fear your terms and your way will not reconcile with my terms and my way.'

His smile chilled her heart. 'Be more specific about your terms, Mrs Forrester.'

She immediately complied. 'I want you...no, I expect you to marry me and to be a good father to our son.'

'Restrict your ambitions to those first three words, my dear, and I'll see what I can do to oblige you.'

Dear Reader

The Meredith Sisters series was launched with *Wedding Night Revenge*, which charted the scandalous exploits of Rachel, the eldest of Edgar and Gloria Meredith's four beautiful daughters. In this ensuing novel, *The Unknown Wife*, Isabel takes her turn to shock polite Society.

The Regency was an era when unmarried ladies of good breeding were expected to act decorously. Unfortunately, fate is abetted by the heroine's intrepidity to decree otherwise. Passionate and principled, Isabel is determined to introduce her son to his father...despite the fact that the man himself has no idea either of them exists.

The third tale features gentle June as the heroine and depicts the fortunes of her early marriage to William Pemberton. June is deemed to be the placid Meredith girl—and so she is, until her contentment is threatened...

The quartet of books will conclude with the youngest sister taking a starring role. Sylvie is a rebellious urchin, more than a match for a charismatic nobleman who arrogantly believes he can tame the silver-haired spitfire with his raw sensuality.

Four young ladies of differing character and interests, but the Meredith sisters are united in their courage and their resolve to win love and happiness. I hope you enjoy reading about how they succeed.

Mary Brendan

Mary Brendan was born in North London and lived there for nineteen years before marrying and migrating north into Hertfordshire. She was grammar-school educated and has been at various times in her working life a personnel secretary for an international oil company, a property developer and a landlady. Presently working part-time in a local library, she dedicates hard-won leisure time to antique-browsing, curries, and keeping up with two lively sons.

Recent titles by the same author:

MR TRELAWNEY'S PROPOSAL
A KIND AND DECENT MAN
THE SILVER SQUIRE
A ROGUISH GENTLEMAN
WEDDING NIGHT REVENGE

Prologue

'I don't want you to go out this evening. Stay home and spend some time with me and our children before they are put to bed.'

The woman might have been deaf for all the attention she paid to those beseeching words or the tall handsome man who had uttered them. Patiently he watched her from his study doorway as she teased abundant dark curls to drape alluringly over her elegant white shoulders. Her head turned this way and that as she assessed her reflected image in an elaborate hallway mirror.

'For pity's sake! Will you look at me? Answer me!'

The beautiful brunette swished about in a rustle of vermilion satin. 'What is wrong with you tonight, Benjamin?' she enquired. 'Is Mrs Smith out of sorts? If you think I will oblige you with playing at happy families because your mistress is indisposed, you are more *stupide* than I imagined.' Her head fell back, exposing a pearly throat, and her low-lidded eyes held a feline intensity as she looked at him. 'Your *chère amie* might be unavailable, but my friend is not,' she purred with insulting indifference. 'Lord Ballantine is due any minute to take me to the opera.'

On hearing who was her escort this evening, her husband approached her with light, rapid steps and gripped a soft arm.

'Your *cicisbeo* can wait…or move on to the next silly strumpet on his list. You are not to be Ballantine's only conquest tonight, I'm sure. As for my mistress, she is not indisposed and would, as ever, be pleased to see me. Which is more than can be said for my lady wife.' He closed his eyes, grimaced regret as an apologetic hand smoothed over pink pressure marks marring her fine skin. 'It is time you and I attempted to put things right between us. The children are old enough now to sense this interminable disharmony. They did not ask to be brought into this world or live in such a bleak atmosphere.'

'The children! Always it is the same. We should live our lives to please the children! Sometimes I wish I had returned to France. Chancing my fate on the tumbrils with my esteemed family might have been preferable to enduring your disgusting touch.'

Her husband smiled thinly, his fingers detached from her arm. 'You? Enduring my disgusting touch? When was that, my dear? Tell me, can you really recall the last time you allowed me into your bed? I'm damned if I can remember enjoying my conjugal rights in five years.'

Beneath an impeccable *maquillage* the woman's face whitened. 'And I am damned, *mon cher,* if I can remember *ever* enjoying my conjugal rights. You have your heir,' she breathed. 'A daughter, too. Leave me be. I have performed all the duty I can or I will for you.' She stepped past him, heading for the street door. By the foot of the stairs her pace faltered. 'Why are you hiding there? Are you spying on your mama? Quick! Up to bed with you, this instant. Tomorrow you are back to school, and not a moment too soon.'

The small boy said nothing, merely fixed the woman with a velvet-brown gaze. She flinched beneath that unwavering, penetrating stare at the same moment his eyes slid past to watch his father through stripes of banister.

'Upstairs with you now!' The woman's voice was strident with unease. 'Do you want the school masters to be told you need a good lesson in manners and discipline?'

The boy's eyes whipped back to his mother, but already he was overlooked, for a butler had portentously materialised in the hallway.

'Lord Ballantine's carriage awaits, ma'am,' the aged servant informed neutrally.

'Méchant...' the woman murmured beneath her breath with a slanting glance at her son. Whilst majestically draping a sable stole about her petite figure, she announced, 'I am the daughter of a count whose august bloodline is centuries old, yet I have a son who is insolent and a husband who is too cowardly to punish him.'

'And I am the son of an earl whose noble ancestry far outstrips yours, yet I have a wife who invites scandal because she acts like a common—' The man's lips compressed into a skewed line as from a corner of his eye he saw his son's fingers clench on oak.

'You are a younger son…a nobody…' she mocked over her shoulder.

The butler hobbled to close the great doors, then merged tactfully into shadow. Just a waft of expensive French perfume hinted at a woman's recent presence.

The man held out a hand. Within a moment crisp cotton was held away from bare feet as the boy padded over cold flags to his father and immediately curved against his hip. Long patrician fingers cradled a fair fragile head close to his waist. When he spoke his voice was hoarse with tears.

'When you are a man, Etienne, choose your wife carefully. Reason and respect must reign. Marrying for loyalty or duty…or even love is unwise. Doing the right thing is often very wrong.'

Chapter One

Had he been anywhere but Ireland those limpid doe eyes attached to his quite solemnly, quite boldly, might have unsettled him. He had coupled with many women, in many countries, but Ireland? Curse it for a dank and dismal hell! He'd never before set foot on a squelching sod of it. And yet...and yet...squinting through lashes rimed with ice, through eyes filmed with cold, he could detect something familiar in the child's face.

The child was still, looking back with quiet instinct, uncaring of the drizzling sleet sleeking his fair hair against his head. The stallion snickered, blew steam at the side of his pink-cheeked face. A hoof batting against the boy's cap, catching ice on the ground, finally took the rider's attention. Moments before the lad had hurtled into the road chasing the hat and laughing, for an icy blast had exposed his tender head. The gangly, tumbling figure had made horse and rider rear back and slew to the right, almost overturning them both.

A dark visage creased fiercely beneath the bite of the elements and its owner's thoughts. But the man was glad now he hadn't bellowed abuse, although the lad deserved scolding. He might have run him down and broken his own neck in the bargain. Brusquely the man flicked, then snapped, leathered fingers at the hat. Obediently it was retrieved with a childish peek at the softening snow. He wasn't afraid. He smiled instead; a faltering curving of lips that arched blond eyebrows into a sleet-spangled fringe.

A broad, brown hand shot out and the cap was knocked clean of its freezing granules.

'You should be careful. I could have knocked you flying. This stallion might have pulped a little chap like you.'

The boy was unabashed, just darting eyes enlivening a complexion drawn with cold. Dark features suddenly swooped close to his as the rider plopped the hat on the child's soaking skull.

'What's his name?' the boy asked, stroking the stallion's flank.

'Storm.'

'What's your name?'

The man seemed as though he might ignore the trembling wistful enquiry, and the small, bone-white fingers still on the flank of his sleek black mount. 'It's polite to say, what is your name, *sir,*' he corrected tersely, but he began to introduce himself anyway. 'Etienne—' The rest was lost to a woman's guttural Irish tone.

'Mother Mary, did I turn me back for one minute to speak with Mrs O'Flaherty and find you gone. Now, what will your ma be sayin' if she finds out all today's mischief...an'— Faith! Look, you're drenched through, so y'are...' A woman clutching at her bonnet and dragging her cloak hard about her stamped over the unyielding street towards them. Grabbing at the lad's hand, she tugged him gently backwards towards the shelter of shop doorways, roaring and making a fist for a cart that drove too snugly by him. There was no more than a sharp stare angled from beneath an awning of bonnet brim to acknowledge the stranger astride his powerful stallion.

Etienne watched as the boy trudged away stabbing the toes of his boots into frozen earth mounds formed by cartwheels. Clods were successfully loosened, tossed off the tip of his boots into the air. Far back in Etienne's mind a childish reminiscence stirred, twitching his thin lips. He reined back, cursing for the hundredth time that he'd not taken the coach for hire at the Fiddle and Flute. But for the blacksmith failing to shoe the lead quick enough for him he would have been travelling in relative comfort towards Waterford. Now he felt unsettled, irritable, and he knew it wasn't just to do with being wet, hungry and cold. An odd feeling that something portentous had occurred wouldn't be shrugged off along with the ice burdening his caped shoulders. Settling his beaver low on his brow, he cursed and kneed the horse forward. It was just a child; an Irish peasant's brat. The boy was nothing to do with him. He'd never before set foot in Ireland, he reminded himself as he sent his mount into a furious gallop.

* * *

'Have you invited me here simply to watch me die of influenza?'

Connor Flinte, Earl of Devane, turned from the slurry obscuring the view through his mullioned window and grinned at the man entering his vast and cosy library. He watched his guest's busy fingers despatching a shower of melting ice from his long dark hair.

Connor's rapid step showed genuine welcome and affection as he closed the space between them to shake hands. 'Is that any way to greet your host? Your long-lost comrade? Some carping gratitude for me fine hospitality, I'm thinking!' Connor chided with liberal Irish charm and intonation.

'Well, you have to admit, Con, this weather is appalling, even for February. Is Ireland always so…so damned *wet?*'

The Earl of Devane quirked an ebony eyebrow at him. 'Wet? Get away with you. This is nothing. You should see it when the rains get here. Seriously, it's good to see you, Etienne. Why did Gallagher not announce you?' Connor frowned at the door. His conscientious butler was nowhere to be seen.

'Oh, I told him not to bother. He seemed a bit flustered. Your porch roof is leaking; as I arrived he was organising the positioning of the buckets with a couple of footmen. It reminded me that the roof of Redgrave Park needs attention.'

'Are you away from here and straight to Redgrave Park? Or have you a mind to stop off in Mayfair?' Connor asked his former comrade-in-arms. 'If you are going to London, I have an errand to beg of you. Would you deliver an urgent letter to my man of business in Cheapside?'

Etienne's expression became decidedly wolfish. 'Oh, I think I might detour through Mayfair en route to Suffolk. And of course I'll be your post boy.'

'How is Lady Avery? Still besotted with you?' Connor asked with a mix of admiration and humour in his voice as he contemplated the beautiful widow who had been this man's mistress for at least half a decade. Plenty of men as wealthy and influential as this one had tried to win her affections and lure her away. Nevertheless she remained steadfastly loyal to her Colonel even, so rumour had it, during those long months that he spent abroad on army duties.

'I believe she's very well,' Etienne replied with a grin. 'Judging from her last *billet-doux,* she'll be delighted to see me. It would be churlish to disappoint her after six months' absence.' His smile sobered. 'I should make it my business to see Miss Caroline Greenwood, too, before I set out to check on Redgrave Park.'

At Connor's enquiring look he elaborated. 'It's time to think about a wife and heirs. Last time I was in town, I paid Miss Greenwood some attention. She seems amenable and is pretty enough. She doesn't blush, stammer or giggle too often. I'll want a decent hostess who is able to conduct herself properly. She's young…about nineteen, I would guess. That apart, she fits the bill.' He chuckled. 'And her parents are more than willing to foot the bill. They've been hinting at a hundred thousand deposited in my bank account as the chit's dowry. Her father has kept regularly in touch. Now I'm home for good I imagine they think I'll take up where I left off. I expect I will.'

'How very romantic,' Connor murmured.

Etienne shot him a look from beneath thick dark brows. 'What's romance got to do with any of it?' he countered in an equally sarcastic vein. 'We've established that Lady Avery is just as fine as ever she was. My marriage won't worry her.'

As though remembering his role as host, Connor indicated his guest should take a seat in a comfy fireside chair, positioned close to glowing coals. He drew his own armchair up to the lofty stone chimneypiece—so enormous was it, he could have put the chair down within the soot-stained cavern. With a weary sigh, Etienne dropped his tall frame into the cushions. One long muscular leg stretched out in negligent ease as his head lolled back to dent soft hide. A dark hand was thrust into a trouser pocket; the other accepted the crystal brandy balloon extended his way. A generous amount of amber liquid rocked alluringly within.

After the two men had sipped appreciatively, taken discreet stock of each other's appearance, and found nothing spectacular to warrant a comment, Etienne turned his thoughts to the thing, or rather person, who did greatly intrigue him. With his dark eyes levelled on Connor, he drew his booted feet across the Aubusson and sat forward, forearms on knees. 'If you want to talk of romance…well, you know I'm not here, risking pneumonia, on your account. Where's that beautiful, tricky wife of yours? It's about time I met her.'

At the mention of Rachel, Connor's hard handsome features softened into a smile. 'She's visiting friends in the village with her sister. And your mother is due any moment.'

'My mother?'

'Claudine's recently been a house guest of the Ormondes. Did you not know?'

Etienne shrugged. 'No. Ormonde is my father's cousin on the paternal side. I've long known my mother has a soft spot for him.'

'Do I detect an element of animosity?'

Etienne's brandy balloon was virtually emptied in one gulp before he replied. 'It makes no difference to me with whom she spends her time. We're not close; you know that. It's only ever been my grandparents cementing us together. And that's another place I must go before I return to Suffolk: to Cambridge to see how they fare. They're both in their eighty-second year, you know.'

Etienne avoided Connor's sympathetic gaze. Eyes the colour of bitter chocolate focused on leaping flames to one side of him as he drained his glass.

'How long can you stay, Etienne?'

Etienne speared him a look. What he read in his friend's face made him chuckle. 'I sense a man desperate for a little masculine company, even if he does have an urgent letter to be taken across the water to his attorney. Are you outnumbered by the ladies, Con?'

Connor looked a little abashed. 'Actually, the letter's not that important, but your company is. I thought, with apologies to Lady Avery, I might impose on you to stay at least a week and act as escort and charming man about town to your mother and my sister-in-law.'

Etienne collapsed into his chair and choked a laugh. 'For God's sake! How long have you been married? Too long for this! Three months—six at the most—is honeymoon time, you know. By my reckoning you've been leg-shackled more than a year and a half.'

'I like my sister-in-law very much, but sometimes a man has a desire to spend time alone with his wife during the day.'

'I do understand,' Etienne soothed him with a grin. 'And true friend that I am, I will be happy to oblige for a week. After that I have a desire to spend some time in London with Lady Avery…you understand?'

Connor grimaced a laughing response.

'Lady Devane must be enchanting,' Etienne said, admiration husky in his voice. 'I can't wait to meet her.'

Isabel Forrester stripped damp gloves from her long slender hands with a grimace. She vigorously shook them to dry them whilst answering a plea from her older sister. 'I will come along to the drawing room, I promise. First I must see how Marcus is. He said he felt poorly this morning before breakfast. I worried about sending him to school at all in this weather. But he has a way of exaggerating when it suits him.' She sighed expressively. 'I wonder if Noreen has brought back more complaints from Father Maguire?'

Rachel agitatedly swung her bonnet by its strings, too excited by her butler's news to pay much attention to her nephew's condition. 'Well, don't be too long. Gallagher says that Colonel Hauke is already arrived. I believe he is very rich and well connected. I've seen him from afar a few times. It was a long while ago, but he made a good impression on me then. In fact, I judged him quite a magnificent specimen of a man.'

'I'm sure, dear,' Isabel humoured her wryly, knowing only too well Rachel was an incurable and persistent matchmaker on her behalf; on the behalf of any unattached lady who found herself in the vicinity of a bachelor of reasonable status and character. 'But only think of the interim in which he has probably deteriorated quite remarkably. Bad teeth, thinning hair…'

'If he *is* balding, you must sell him a pot of your hair restorer. He will propose before the day is out.'

Isabel smiled at that. She had concocted a hair lotion from her physic garden for a new mother in the village. The woman was delighted when her hair loss decreased. Isabel thought it more likely to be due to her health strengthening now the child was being weaned than any miracle cure derived from rosemary and lavender.

Aware that her husband was even now awaiting her presence in the library to welcome to Wolverton Manor one of his oldest friends, Rachel Flinte, Countess of Devane, relinquished her cloak and hat to the waiting footman. With a toss of her golden hair, followed by a pat to subdue several buoyant curls, she was off in the direction of the library.

'Ma'am? It's dinnertime, ma'am. Are you awake?'

The harsh Irish brogue grazed Isabel's dreams, bringing her to bleary consciousness. She blinked herself awake to see Noreen Smith's freckled, frowning face close to hers. With a rub to her heavy eyes, she turned over on to her elbow and gazed at the wall clock. It was close to chiming the hour of eight. Isabel groaned.

Noreen's rusty red brows formed twin arches under which her eyes swivelled. A hiss of caution pushed through her pout. Isabel gleaned from these facial gymnastics that the maidservant deemed her reluctance to dine bad manners.

'Guests, ma'am…from England,' Noreen succinctly explained with a meaningful nod. Noreen was Rachel's servant. She had come overseas with the newly wed Countess of Devane and remained steadfastly loyal to her mistress. Isabel was virtually a stranger to her, although Noreen had served the Meredith family for more than a decade.

'It'll take but a moment to have you ready,' Noreen announced briskly. 'And no need to fret over the young master. He's tired out and in bed. He's been helping my Sam in the stables…' Noreen's lips pressed together. Her husband was too inclined to indulge the fatherless little mite. Busily she tipped warm water into a bowl.

Isabel's blue dimity gown received a shake to disperse the creases as she peered into her closet. Emerald silk was twitched this way and that.

'Your sister has on that new cerise satin,' Noreen volunteered helpfully. 'Sure an' it makes her look like a princess. And Mrs Hauke not long ago arrived with just one maid with her. All wet and windswept, wasn't they, but the lady full of smiles and thanks. Kind and gracious she is, that's what I'm thinking. She's dressed in lavender silk.'

Isabel splashed her complexion with warm water, then held a towel at her face before she looked at her reflection in the small glass on the washstand. Solemnly she inspected unusually pale skin and fragile-looking features. A spiralling curl of unruly beige hair was pushed back from her cheek. Cerise satin would never suit her colouring, and her looks were hardly princess-like. Her sister, Rachel fitted the bill on both counts. She watched the small mouth in the mirror twist ruefully. So Mrs Hauke was newly arrived but already dressed and ready to dine. The woman must be famished! The towel was dropped to the washstand. 'Rachel is wearing her new pink satin? Then I'll wear the emerald gown, Noreen.'

'I'm so glad you braved the vile weather Colonel Hauke, and are arrived in time for dinner. Connor tells me you have agreed to stay a while. In fact, Connor has told me much about you.'

'Has he, indeed? I hope most is good.'

'There was nothing bad, I swear,' Rachel laughingly insisted. 'But then I suppose my husband must be diplomatic lest you retaliate with tales of his misdemeanours.' She slid a flirtatious look into humorous, deep brown eyes. *Do hurry, Isabel, for Heaven's sake—he is the most gorgeous man!* raced through her bubbling mind. 'I suppose there were some concerning Connor?' At her suave guest's quizzical look, she explained, 'Misdemeanours. No doubt you and Connor weren't always angels whilst soldiering far from home.'

'Nothing dreadful springs to mind, ma'am, I assure you,' Etienne smoothly reassured whilst mentally congratulating himself on telling the truth. Far from being dreadful, indulging in sin far from home was usually vastly pleasurable. Nevertheless, changing the subject seemed expedient as he scanned the lovely rosy face turned up to his. 'I'm disappointed I missed the wedding.'

'Oh, you weren't alone in that, sir,' Rachel informed him on a shy smile. 'The only people

present were Connor and me and two wit-
nesses. Even our parents missed the wedding.
But it's a shame you were not able to attend
our reception. We held that a few weeks later
and it was a perfect occasion. Connor tried to
contact you but, alas, you were again abroad.'

Etienne noticed the countess's hands nervously toying with her fan. She was afraid he
might mention he recalled her juvenile antics
that had rocked polite society. At nineteen she
had callously jilted Connor, then six years
later, when deemed by all to be on the shelf,
she'd agreed to marry the newly ennobled Earl
of Devane. Connor had never stopped loving
her despite the torment she'd put him through.
'I'm glad…very glad that all turned out so
right for you both. At one time it seemed it
never would.'

'Yes, for a long, long time it seemed it never
would.' Rachel tilted her head to meet his dark
eyes watching her closely. Of course this man
knew all her momentous romantic history: that
she had hurt Connor, brought him to despair.
He probably also knew that through those six
barren years without Connor she had jilted
other men. She couldn't be sure that beneath

the colonel's charming exterior he wasn't disgusted and disapproving of his friend's choice of wife. Not that she expected him to like her on such short acquaintance. Yet she felt that after chatting to him for barely twenty minutes she was already on the way to liking him. The colour was beginning to burn in her cheeks, for no reason other than she didn't want Colonel Hauke to judge her on past follies too harshly or too soon. Her gaze focused on the broad muscular chest close by. She found a neutral topic of conversation. 'Why, Colonel Hauke, that waistcoat you have on looks uncommonly similar to one that Connor has. I believe you must have the same tailor. Connor swears Goldman and Stein of Draper's Lane are the finest outfitters in England.'

Etienne glanced down at the figured silk adorning his chest. Then he looked at the woman frowning at it simply because she was embarrassed. It had been arrogant of him eight years ago to think he had the right to meddle because he was Connor's closest friend. And it was sheer luck that Connor and his beloved had not discovered what he'd tried to do. Lady Devane seemed a charming woman; Etienne was beginning to like her. Thank God no harm had been done.

'You're very observant, ma'am. Actually, it is your husband's waistcoat. My packing case is stuck somewhere between here and the Fiddle and Flute. Connor kindly loaned me some clothes so I might appear at dinner dry and uncrumpled.' He opened the black jacket to fully exhibit the pearl-grey waistcoat and the rest of his sartorially splendid muscular frame. 'Everything I stand up in tonight is courtesy of your excellent husband.'   Rachel glanced modestly at the impressive torso on display. Her blush deepened with her involuntary husky laugh. 'And very well it fits and suits you, sir,' she murmured. 'You and Connor are of the same size.'

'What are you flaunting at my wife, Hauke?' Connor demanded teasingly as he crossed the room towards them.

'Just your superb taste in tailoring, Con… what else?'

'Take no notice of what he says, Rachel, he is a philanderer and not to be trusted with the ladies.'

'I think he seems very trustworthy.' Rachel declined her husband's advice with a cheeky smile.

Etienne acknowledged her championship with an inclination of his dark head, a glint of chestnut enriching a lock of hair that slunk on to his forehead. 'Many thanks, my lady.'

'Oh, enough of this *my lady,*' Rachel squeaked, feeling oddly more flirtatious now that her husband was here at her side. She looked about and her eyes settled on Mrs Hauke, comfortably ensconced in a chair by the fire, sipping a glass of sweet ratafia. 'I am going to have a chat with your mother, Colonel, to quiz her over any *on-dits* circulating among the *ton*. If after a few more minutes my sister is not arrived, I shall go and fetch her down myself before we all expire from hunger.'

'I'm sorry to be late. I'm here now, Rachel,' soothed a melodic voice from behind.

Chapter Two

'How old is your son, Mrs Forrester?'

Isabel carefully put down her soup spoon. 'Just seven, Mrs Hauke.'

'And his name?'

'Marcus.'

'Ah, that's a fine name for a boy. Is Marcus named after his papa? Is he already abed or is he permitted to come downstairs later? I should like to meet him.'

'He is already in bed for he is up early for school in the mornings.' Even now, with many years and many miles separating her from prying eyes and malicious tongues in England, Isabel felt uncomfortable discussing her personal life.

A vague French intonation to Claudine Hauke's voice gave it a husky musical tone. They had chatted over trivialities whilst the first course of game soup was served and Isabel had cheerfully added her complaints to Claudine's concerning the appalling weather they were experiencing. Now the conversation was becoming disconcertingly intimate, although Isabel realised nothing sinister lurked in Claudine's dinner-table chatter. The woman seemed utterly charming and keen to be congenial.

A glance through scintillating candlesticks and spears of flame settled on Connor and Rachel, engrossed in conversation with their urbane guest. Peals of laughter were more frequent than the chime of busy cutlery from that side of the table.

An air of amity was pervading the atmosphere. Isabel anticipated Claudine asking more questions and ruining the harmony. As a diversionary tactic she asked one of her own. 'Are you well acquainted with the Ormondes? Rachel tells me you have been staying with the family. I met them once, about three months ago, just after I arrived in Ireland. I found them agreeable people.'

The Ormondes were the Devanes' neighbours. Lord Ormonde was a widower who lived with his aged mother and two teenage daughters in a vast and draughty fortress. Rachel and Isabel had received an invitation to partake of luncheon with them, but once within Ormonde Castle's perishing walls, had not stayed long enough to dine for fear of risking frostbite before they received one warming morsel.

'Lord Ormonde is a second cousin of my late husband's,' Claudine happily explained. 'When we were married he officiated as one of the ushers. After that we lost touch for a while…until my husband's death following an injury at Waterloo. Vincent attended his funeral. The following year Vincent lost his wife. We have since grown quite close.' Claudine folded elegant hands on the table, preparing to gossip. 'Vincent visits me in Chelsea and brings his daughters to enjoy the season. I think he hopes one—the eldest and comeliest—might eventually attract a husband. We have a nice time together. When one is widowed life can easily become empty and lonely. Of course, you must know that.' Sympathy resonated in her tone. '*C'est tragique* that you should be left with a small son to rear! A boy needs a papa. *Le pauvre petit!* Did your husband succumb to an illness? Was he still young?'

'He was a soldier. Quite young...' Isabel whispered unsteadily, wondering how on earth she had been slack-witted enough to allow the conversation to circle back to her own situation. She quickly, firmly banned any further mention of the subject. 'I'm sorry, I do not like to talk of it.'

'*Naturellement!* So sorry!' Claudine sibilantly whispered. She patted comfortingly on Isabel's slender hand resting on glossy yew. 'Sometimes people like to talk. Vincent likes to talk of his wife and the fine times they shared before her illness—'

'Ormonde likes the sound of his own voice. It seems to be a contagious affliction. I fear you've been spending far too much time with him, *cherie.*'

Startled by the harsh interruption, Claudine eventually choked out a squeak of embarrassed laughter, but her cheeks were rosily tinged beneath her powdery *maquillage.* For all her indignation there was real hurt in her dark, almond-shaped eyes. 'I assure you, *madame* that

I intended no offence.' She shot an angry look at her son.

Isabel tilted her head to take a glance past candles at her unexpected champion. She felt shocked, not simply because Colonel Hauke had publicly rebuked his mother and come to her rescue, but because something about his voice seemed familiar.

The Colonel's eyes found Isabel's across the table, and held them with an intensity that kept her transfixed. Slowly his mouth moved; it was a private smile and evoked quite a mix of emotion to roil within Isabel.

Tonight, on being introduced, this man had behaved towards her with impeccable politeness…nothing more. Once seated, Colonel Hauke had glanced at her and smiled courteously, just the once, before resuming his conversation with Rachel. Isabel had felt oddly wounded by his indifference, for on meeting him a wistful feeling had involuntarily taken root in her breast. Rachel was right. He was magnificent; an impressive, imposing man, and a fine catch. He was not lordly, he was not conventionally good-looking, but he was vastly appealing and instinctively she knew women wanted him. And such eligible bachelors were not for her. They were for her sisters. Isabel Forrester, née Meredith, was a woman wreathed in secrets and shadows, as was her son. Such potent men were best ignored lest they caused her to become restless and dissatisfied with her lot. Still, she'd wished the Colonel had looked at her with more interest. Now he was; she had his undivided attention and a frisson of excitement came tempered with nervousness.

Earlier, when Connor had taken her and his wife into dinner, Isabel had watched the broad, elegantly clad back of Colonel Hauke leading his mother to dine. Suddenly she had felt the humiliating burden of her sister and brother-in-law's generosity. Not only were she and her son allowed to freely board and lodge beneath their roof but, on an occasion such as this, Rachel would also share her wonderful husband with her younger sister, so Isabel could briefly imagine how it felt to be cherished, protected and loved by a fine gentleman. Why it should rankle so this evening, when usually she allowed Connor's solicitude barely to unsettle her, she could not say.

Her eyes dropped away from that earth-dark gaze trained on her. 'Are you acquainted with the Fitzgeralds, Mrs Hauke?' Isabel pleasantly enquired, signalling gracious forgiveness. 'I have become quite friendly with Clodagh Fitzgerald and her brother Liam. They have a dairy farm to the north of here.'

After dinner Isabel stationed herself alone by the French windows. She gazed into the blackness, and was not at all surprised to hear footsteps cracking closer over polished boards. Her heart beat uncomfortably fast, yet obliquely she realised she had separated from the others in the hope he might come over and speak privately to her.

'I'm sorry about that.'

'I'm not sure why, sir. I don't recall you behaving in a way that warrants an apology.' Isabel chewed at her bottom lip, immediately regretting her petulance. She had sought to be solitary, sensing it would lure him. Now she was being silly in regretting her ploy's effectiveness and churlish in abusing his good manners. He wasn't obliged to apologise for his mother's inquisitiveness when the woman herself had already done so.

She remained staring through glass at spectral shrubbery silhouetted by a full moon's silvery bloom. The knot of tension lodged in her breast tightened mercilessly.

The Colonel lounged back against the doorframe to one side of her. She had but to shift her gaze a fraction to look into his tough, hardboned face or run a shy eye over that solid, athletic physique. She wanted to look at him. He had a face that was intriguing, kept one looking long after etiquette deemed it polite.

His features were rugged, savaged by the elements, not conventionally handsome by any means. He was not Adonis-like as was Connor, with his raven hair and beautifully proportioned and symmetrical face. But the Colonel had an equally commanding presence that had kept her mesmerised like a fool when they had been first introduced. It was the slight amusement skewing his sensual mouth as she stood entranced, her hand still in his, that had finally jolted her to her senses and speedily sent her, chagrined, to the opposite side of the dining table to claim a seat close to his mother.

'You looked, still look, as though my mother might have upset you. She has a tendency to be tactlessly prying.' The Colonel's tone was cool and crisp. He was acknowledging her chilly reception.

'I took no offence, I assure you.' Isabel managed a conciliatory smile. He must think her moodiness odd. It wasn't his fault that, after barely a few hours in his company, she found him...unsettling. She added lightly, 'I like your mother; even on such a short acquaintance. I believe she sincerely wants to show sympathy for others' misfortune.'

That comment elicited a sardonic laugh from him. 'She would far rather concentrate on a stranger's calamities than her own, it's true. Have we met before?'

Startled, Isabel looked properly at him. 'No...why do you say that?' With her heart suddenly racing, she wondered if he had sensed, as she had, an odd hint of something familiar. She knew it was ridiculous; if this man came into one's life, the memory of it ought be indelible.

He shrugged. 'I thought when your sister and Connor were engaged years ago we might have come into contact socially.'

Imperceptibly Isabel relaxed. 'I don't recall such an occasion.'

He smiled. 'Neither do I and I would, I'm sure.'

'You're too kind, sir,' Isabel shot back with just a trace of acid sharpening the honey of her tone. It still rankled that earlier he had virtually overlooked her. She shifted her gaze back to the window, hoping he would go now…no, hoping she could make him stay, just a while longer. A thirst for his calm, debonair person had parched her throat. Besides, a stubborn desire to keep him there so she could match his insouciance was bedevilling her. Talking about the food they had eaten seemed an obvious mundane topic. So she remarked on the diversity of the courses, informing him of the way that neighbours shared produce. He readily agreed that dinner had been exceedingly fine and a cooperative attitude amongst farmers was a most welcome and sensible situation.

Isabel liked listening to his drawling baritone voice; it had a slightly somnolent quality. But it was cultured English, very different from Claudine's intonation. She found another topic of conversation. 'Your mother has a very pleasant French accent, sir. Was your father French, too?'

The Colonel gave her a rueful smile, then a concise account of his lineage. 'No. He was an English captain in the Kings Own Dragoons. My mother was born into the French nobility...hard to believe, I know, when she displays such common inquisitiveness. Her father was a count and she was fortunate to find herself on the right side of the Channel when the French Revolution began. Naturally she accepted refuge with those English friends who had been her hosts. Her mother, father and brother, together with numerous aunts, uncles and cousins, were lost to the guillotine. I never knew any of them.'

Isabel was momentarily stunned into openly staring at him. Her eyes clung to his impassive profile in amazement and sympathy.

Etienne's eyes swooped to hers and were equally arrested. On first meeting her he'd been surprised by her sweet, ethereal looks. Connor had mentioned earlier that his wife's widowed sister and nephew were staying with them and, for some reason, he had imagined her to be a pleasant, matronly young woman.

Isabel Forrester was anything but that. Despite some sense of recognition niggling at the back of his mind, what dominated his thoughts was that he could not possibly have met this woman before and not remembered the occasion. He would never forget such an exquisite face…those lovely eyes. He told himself that the most likely explanation was that he'd seen her likeness somewhere. The inner vision he couldn't dispel was of a solemn sylph with a garland of ivy calming her curls, reposing in a halcyon woodland glade with elves and fairies scattered about her tiny feet. It was probably a book illustration he'd appreciated. The graceful nymph he was now discreetly admiring had replaced the garland of greenery with a green ribbon that almost matched the colour of her entrancing eyes. Tresses that looked too luxuriant to be tamed with just one thin strip of emerald satin were confined at her nape in a coil as thick as his fist. The colour of her hair was unusual, a shade that merged brown and gold to give a fair shade of tan.

He had been impressed by her sister's looks. This woman was equally as beautiful, but very different. The Countess of Devane's china-

blue eyes and golden hair would find immediate favour with most red-blooded males if
they could draw their eyes from her lush figure. Isabel Forrester had a more subtle allure:
petite, willowy...almost too slender. But her
silk gown had a disturbing tendency to sway
and cling in exactly the right places as she
moved.

When Connor had informed him earlier in
the day that his sister-in-law was rearing her
son on her own, an unusual gravity to his
friend's tone had conveyed that no further information would be forthcoming. Etienne had
respectfully heeded that tacit warning and the
subject was closed. Perhaps he should have
taken it upon himself to caution his mother not
to probe. In a purely selfish way he was glad
she had, for now he knew a little more about
Isabel Forrester. She had a son of seven years
of age and her husband had been a soldier.

From her son's age he guessed she would
have been married at least approaching eight
years ago. Thus she must have married young,
perhaps at about the time of Connor and
Rachel's aborted nuptials. When had her husband died? Recently? No. She would still be

in her widow's weeds. He wanted to know more, and a wry inner smile acknowledged the unseemly inquisitiveness he had condemned in his mother. Why did any of it matter to him? Soon he would be in Mayfair with other women to think about. He had a passionate mistress and a prospective wife awaiting his arrival.

Etienne's introspection was interrupted by a softly horrified voice. 'You have lost so many relatives to the Terror! That's awful.'

'I never knew them. They were quitting this life just as I arrived in it. My father's parents are still thriving. I have one set of grandparents.' There was a flash of rueful humour softening his eyes as he murmured, 'Sometimes I think they're more than enough kin to be getting along with.' After a pause he said, 'But I should have liked to know my French family.'

'Yes, of course!' Isabel agreed earnestly. 'It is not right that a child be deprived of his relatives.'

'At dinner your sister was saying that she misses England and her friends and family there.' Etienne angled a look at the Earl and Countess of Devane chatting with his mother on a settee drawn close to blazing logs. 'I imagine the Earl might be persuaded to go to London for the season. Will you go too?'

Isabel shrugged in a passably casual way. 'Ireland suits me very well. If my sister and her husband do go to England, I might stay here a while.' She was aware of dark eyes watching, of the silence indicating he was waiting for her to explain such an odd declaration. Why on earth would she stay at her brother-in-law's residence, far from home and family, once her sister was gone? She felt obliged to offer an explanation and then wished she had remained quiet. 'My son is at school in the village. I should not like to disrupt his studies. He has made friends...and some progress...' she added weakly.

'He attends a local village school?' Isabel was aware of the subdued surprise in his tone. Her status as sister-in-law to an earl would make most people assume her son enjoyed enough reflected privilege to be instructed by a good tutor at home until he was despatched to a reputable boarding school. That would be customary for the nephew of a wealthy gentleman.

Etienne watched her expression, watched her nervous hands smooth along her silk gown in a way that tautened emerald silk across her thighs. It was all the more erotic for being innocent and unconscious. She was agitated. Possibly that was due to the fact that it embarrassed her to admit she could not afford a proper education for her son. Perhaps her husband had died and left her in a parlous financial state. She didn't look shabby genteel: her clothes were superb. He knew of old that Connor could be altruistic. With his wife's sister he would be unstintingly, unconditionally generous. If she wanted her son educated, Flinte would pay without a qualm. And where was her father in all this? Edgar Meredith was surely comfortably off. Should he not be supporting his grandson? If the boy was being taught locally he was probably hobnobbing with the offspring of the lower middle-classes or tenant farmers; people with intelligence enough to desire for their children more than they had scratched from life, yet they were hardly his peers.

'It is an age since we sat down to dine together, then when we do you tell me off for a conversation. So, I shall try to stay quiet and please you. What have you been doing, *cheri?* And where are you next going? Am I invited to come and stay at Redgrave Park with you?'

Etienne acknowledged his mother's blunt interruption with a chill smile. 'You must try harder than that, *Maman,* if you sincerely wish to please me. No, you can't come to Redgrave Park. I'm not yet returning to Suffolk. I have business in the city. If you're at a loose end, perhaps Vincent might like you to stay a while in Ireland,' he suggested caustically.

A Gallic shrug contoured Claudine's elegant white shoulders. '*Peut-être;* but this Ireland is so cold and wet. Sleet…snow…rain…gales and all in the one day.' She slanted a crafty look at her son from beneath lowered lashes. 'Perhaps I know why you are going first to London. Is it business concerning a certain Miss Caroline Greenwood?' Claudine sent Isabel a conspiratorial look. 'Before I left Chelsea I heard a rumour. I hope you are not expecting your *maman* to scour the *gazettes* to find out for sure. Are you to publicly announce your engagement soon, *mon fils?* If so, I must tell your sister. Monique will be cross if she hears of it second-hand or reads it in *The Times.*'

Clearly annoyed that his private business was being discussed, Etienne shoved back the thick chestnut hair that flopped close to his eyes. A flinty look encompassed Isabel. She automatically smiled at him in a dazed way.

'Should I decide to get married, you will be among the first to know, *cherie,* I promise.'

For a moment Isabel was sure he was about to immediately excuse himself. An impatient stride had already taken him away from her. He hesitated, then angled a look at her. 'Connor tells me I must stay a while to keep you company. Do you like to ride?'

Had Isabel not been stunned on learning this man was virtually betrothed, she would have felt very insulted by such blunt honesty. But she simply replied, 'Yes, I like to ride.'

'Good; tomorrow we should take the air together.' With that and a neat bow he walked away.

Chapter Three

'Sam says he didn't have no learnin', 'cos a groom don't need no learnin' 'cept about nourishing horses and doctoring their aches and pains. I want to work with Sam. So why do I need to be learnt?'

Isabel closed her eyes in exasperation at her young son's excruciating pronouncement. Marcus was spending too much time with Sam Smith, yet how could she deny him the happiness he gained from the groom's company? Her lonely son idolised any man who showed him a little time and affection.

The cockney groom's wife, fetching coats and hats, pursed her lips in vexation on hearing her spouse's rough wisdom repeated. Not that Marcus was fibbing; Noreen had been regaled with the same blunt theories on book-learning from her husband. With her cheeks flaming red enough to rival her hair, Noreen promised herself that, like it or not, Sam Smith would get a lesson himself later, when she had him alone.

'You will go to school, Marcus, and you will put on your coat and button it through. It's cold outside despite the sunshine.'

Marcus met his mother's instructions with a sulky glower, then glanced at Noreen, hoping for an ally. Noreen kept her face averted and her eyes concealed behind ginger lashes.

'And I have a headache.' Marcus pressed a small hand to his brow in a way his mother might solicitously do when he complained of feeling poorly.

'Put on your coat, Marcus,' Isabel ordered, trying to slide one of his evasive arms into a sleeve. 'Goodness! Do we have to have this very pantomime so often? If you refuse to attend Father Maguire's school, I shall have to get Mr O'Dare to come and teach you again at home.' The threat lacked conviction. The gaunt-faced nervous tutor she had employed shortly after their arrival in Ireland was unlikely to agree to come back. The man had seemed as intimidated by her boisterous, demanding son as he had seemed impressed at the prospect of tutoring the Earl of Devane's nephew. The only reason the man had persevered with the *unruly child* was because Connor paid him more than the going rate.

'I shall just run away again if you bring him back. I told you I don't like sums!' Marcus snarled.

'Hello, who is this young man who might run away rather than do his sums?' teased an amused, accented voice.

Isabel smiled distractedly at Claudine Hauke as the woman descended the gracious sweep of oaken stairs. Claudine was garbed in a bottle-green riding habit cut from fine velvet and edged in sable. Its excellent style neatly hugged her figure. For a woman possibly past fifty she had an enviably girlish shape, Isabel thought as she watched the French woman settle a matching hat atop her head and secure the strings. Mrs Hauke obviously had the wherewithal to purchase herself beautiful clothes.

Claudine approached Marcus with a curious smile. The boy looked back with a similarly inquisitive expression.

'Say hello to Mrs Hauke, Marcus,' Isabel instructed as she led him gently closer to their guest.

Claudine inclined towards the boy to scan his solemn fair face for a few moments. 'So! At last we meet. Where have you been hiding, young man? For days I have been looking forward to seeing you.' Claudine straightened and looked at Isabel. 'He is so beautiful and very like my grandchildren. My daughter, Monique, has twins: a boy and a girl just turned three years old. Sophie's hair is as blond...' one of Claudine's hands ruffled Marcus's fine flaxen mop '...and Phillipe's eyes are as round and bright but all brown, not tinged with green as are yours, young man. Neither do they yet spark with such mischief. But he can be a proper scamp, so his mama says. Are you off to school now, Marcus?'

Marcus kept his features mutinous a moment longer. A smile suddenly smoothed the pucker between his brows. 'Yes, ma'am,' he said politely.

'*C'est très bien.* A young chap must be good and learn his lessons, then one day he shall lead a useful life.'

'Grooms are useful. Horses think so.'

'Indeed,' his mother gently concurred. 'But first a groom must go to school in case...in case he changes his profession and wishes instead to study law or medicine. He might even decide to be a banker in the city like his grandpapa.'

'My grandpapa doesn't like me so I shan't be a banker. Perhaps I might be a sailor,' Marcus chirped up, shoving his arms helpfully into his coat and obediently buttoning the garment. 'Sam says he would have liked to be a Jack Tar who went to war on the *Victory* and killed lots of horrid Frenchies.'

'Your grandpapa does like you,' Isabel huskily corrected. She grimaced at Claudine in a way that conveyed her embarrassment and apologised for her son's gauche xenophobic remark.

Claudine merely shrugged off the insult to her countrymen. 'You are a good patriotic boy, Marcus. I have little liking myself for a lot of those Frenchies.' The woman's voice was gruff with emotion and Isabel recalled what Colonel Hauke had told her about his mother's family being assassinated by insurgents. It didn't seem the right time to offer condolences.

'Come along now,' Noreen diplomatically broke into the silence and chivvied her young charge. 'If we're not soon away you'll be late for registration, so y'will, Master Marcus. The coach is waiting. You won't want to be late, at all. The Father will be cross, so he will.'

Isabel stooped, managed to skim a kiss against her son's fine fair hair as he whisked past. 'Be good!' A mother's anxious call followed his small figure as it hurtled down the steps. Samuel Smith helped Marcus to climb aboard his uncle's sumptuous coach.

'He's a lucky boy to arrive at school in such style,' Claudine remarked lightly, seeming recovered from her melancholy.

'Yes…most of the other pupils walk.'

'I am surprised…' Claudine tactfully curtailed her observation.

Isabel knew she meant to say she was surprised that her son attended such an establishment at all.

After a short pause Claudine concluded, 'Marcus could learn his lessons at home, *non?*'

'He did for a while. He…it didn't suit him. He is easily bored. It's best he is with his friends.'

'He looks like his papa,' Claudine stated softly.

Isabel swished about to dart a startled glance at Claudine. 'What makes you say that?' she demanded in a single breath.

'He doesn't look like you, although he is fair and handsome with green in his eyes,' Claudine reasoned. 'I suspect he has his father's face. Am I right? Does he resemble his papa?'

'I imagine he does,' Isabel admitted faintly.

Claudine Hauke gave a soft laugh. 'I have learnt my lesson and shall stop now. No more unseemly inquisitiveness or my son will again tell me off. He quite gave me the megrims the night we arrived with such a cruel set-down. I have the ache here still.' She rubbed a small hand across her brow. 'A brisk ride in the fresh air always blows out the cobwebs. He is to meet me at the stables before breakfast. It looks a glorious morning. Will you join us today?'

'No…thank you,' Isabel quickly refused the offer, as she had every other offer to ride. The Haukes had been guests now for several days but still a residue of indignation lingered that

Colonel Hauke might feel obliged to spend time with her. Isabel more closely examined Claudine. The woman did look rather pale. 'I can prepare you a headache remedy, if you like.'

'Are you a herbalist, Isabel?' Claudine enquired with a final press to the crease between her eyes.

'I have always been interested in herbal cures and my mother was grateful for my tending to the physic garden when I lived at home at Windrush. It is a useful plot when one has a family of four girls and a deal of female complaints as well as usual aches and pains.'

'In France, once upon a time, dispensing such cures brought one under suspicion of witchcraft.' Claudine clucked her tongue. 'That was a silly story to bring to your attention! Of course, we are all now more civilised about such things.'

'I know it's true. But for a century or so separating me from such ignorance, I might have been branded and burned at the stake.' Isabel delivered the comment with good humour.

'On that terrifying note I think I must leave you.' Claudine pulled on her leather gloves, smoothing them with long strokes. She glanced about the hallway. 'Have you seen my son this morning?' At Isabel's quick shake of the head, the French woman added, 'I suppose I should venture outside; he might already be waiting for me in the stables and get cross and ride off if he has to kick his heels too long on my account.'

Isabel hadn't seen Claudine's son this morning. But she had at dinner yesterday evening when he again asked her to join him on a morning constitutional. She had no intention of letting arrogant Colonel Hauke—the conceit of the man!—escort or entertain her during his week-long sojourn in Ireland with his friend.

Besides, today Isabel had a perfectly reasonable excuse to decline the Haukes' invitation to ride with them: she had already made arrangements to accompany Clodagh to Waterford should market day turn out dry. Against all odds, it had. She went to the large vestibule window to examine the landscape and scour the skies. It was while she was contemplating the vagaries of the Irish climate that the Colonel appeared.

Without once turning her head to look properly at him, Isabel was aware of him leisurely descending the stairs almost as soon as one mirror-bright boot hit the top tread. She knew that one of his hands was gliding along the banister while the other grasped a riding crop close to a buff-breeched leg. She knew that his dark brown hair was tinted auburn by slanting sunbeams entering through the high hall windows. She knew exactly the moment he became aware of her motionless presence half-screened by the deep window embrasure. She gazed sightlessly through glass, pondering whether to remain where she was, engrossed in the scenery, thus presenting him with an opportunity to discreetly take evasive action. She held her ground. Let him choose.

Within a moment he had joined her in the stone recess. A lean hand lounged, close to her head, against the window's sturdy frame. He greeted her with a polite, 'Good morning.'

Isabel felt her stomach flip at his closeness and hated herself for it. She was acting like an excited schoolgirl with a silly crush, not a woman in her mid-twenties with a seven-year old son and no desire to ever again be in thrall to a man. Especially one whose betrothal was soon to be announced, she wryly reminded herself. She politely returned his greeting; a congenial smile accompanied it for good measure. Then when the silence lengthened and they both appeared fascinated by clouds scudding at some speed across a washed winter sky, Isabel felt a betraying rush of colour to her cheeks. She felt annoyed with herself for again being far too conscious of his presence. A moment ago she had stolen a fleeting glance at him and held her breath in an instinctive response to his appearance. It was ridiculous!

'Your mother has just gone to the stables to meet you.' The comment was casually delivered. 'She was anxious not to keep you waiting, in case you got impatient and made off alone.'

'I see; she's made me sound like some sort of grumpy ogre.'

'No, not at all.' Isabel was keen not to exacerbate any tension that existed between mother and son. She had sensed on several occasions that all was not harmonious between them.

He said nothing, but another furtive glance at his profile showed her that a smile was tilting the edge of his lips. She guessed it was a reaction to her diplomacy, her instinctive desire to be nice. Perhaps immediate compliance was something he took for granted in people. But she wasn't one of his foot soldiers!

She turned to him fully, challengingly. 'Is your mother correct? Are you a grumpy ogre, Colonel Hauke?'

'Sometimes…' he agreed impenitently, with a thoughtful nod. Humour was apparent in his voice and made her bridle further.

Isabel glanced back through the window, no more than a lift of her finely drawn brows deigning to respond to that.

'Don't you want to know when that is or why?'

'When? Why?' Isabel obliged him, honeying her tone with irony.

'It's when I can't get my own way. And it's because I'm disappointed about something. As I am now.'

'Are you expecting me to want you to explain?'

'Of course.'

'Please explain,' she duly said, all sweetness.

'In a moment, if I ask you if you'll come riding with me, you'll decline again and leave me feeling that I haven't got my own way and that I'm disappointed. It's probably best that I don't ask.'

Isabel subdued a smile. 'Please don't take the Earl's instruction to spend time with me too seriously, sir. I'd hate your attempts at chivalry to become an ordeal...for us both.'

'I knew I shouldn't have said that. It was quite definitely a stupid utterance. It's true your brother-in-law asked me to keep you and my mother company this week but that's not why I'm asking. I'm asking for me, not for him. I'd like you to ride with me.'

'I'm sorry; I have other arrangements already made for this morning.'

'Which are?'

'You really are quite alarmingly unseemly in your persistence, Colonel Hauke. If you must know, I am meeting a friend. It is market day in Waterford and we are going shopping.'

'It's still early; there's plenty of time for shopping later.'

'Did your mother never teach you, sir, that you should accept rejection philosophically and gracefully?'

'Is that what you teach your son?'

Isabel's flirtatious smile faltered and she turned away from him. A silence laden with tension terminated with a whispered, 'Yes, that's what I tell him.'

'Where is he?'

'He's just left for school.'

'I'm sorry I missed him. I know you're not up and dressed at this ungodly hour to see me off on a morning gallop. Do you see him off to school every day?'

'Yes, of course.'

'Yes, of course...' the Colonel repeated softly.

'Is there something wrong with that?' Isabel demanded defensively.

'No, nothing at all is wrong with that. I should have liked it had my mother seen me off to school. Once or twice a year as I was packed off to board would have sufficed. You're a good mother, obviously.' It was a statement requiring no response and, with a curt bow of his dark head and a shove of a hand that propelled him sharply back from the window, he was gone.

Isabel was still standing there, feeling confused, when Connor and Rachel joined her. Her brother-in-law, as usual, looked darkly handsome in riding clothes and her sister epitomised elegance in her navy blue outfit with gold buttons and fancy braid frogging.

'Go ahead and saddle Willow for me, I want to have a chat with Bella. I've hardly seen her in days,' Rachel told her dashing husband.

Isabel could tell from Rachel's purposeful look what was coming next and pre-empted her with a casual, 'Yes, Colonel Hauke is attractive, yes, he is quite charming and, yes, I think he would make a good catch. Which is just as well for a certain Miss Caroline Greenwood. His mother let slip earlier in the week that he is on the verge of proposing to her.'

Rachel groaned. 'Not her! Heavens! I wonder if Connor knows? He's not said.'

'Connor might not have thought it worth mentioning,' Isabel suggested. 'Why do you say ''her'' like that?'

'Oh she's so...so insipid and her parents, especially her mother—who, by the by, looks like a horse, and not a thoroughbred at that—are quite awful social climbers. It is well known that Mrs Greenwood is title-digging for Caroline. I'll be surprised if he marries her. I think he has better taste.'

Isabel shrugged, but privately hoped Rachel was right. Why would such a man need to marry into a vulgar family? Unless... 'Perhaps he is in love,' she mentioned over her shoulder as she went to fetch her coat and hat from the hall chair.

Rachel gave a snort of laughter. 'Well, if he is, I must have misjudged his character. Her family have money...lots of it...from coal, I think. But Connor says Hauke has pots of the stuff himself and more to come when his uncle and his grandfather pass on. He is due to inherit from both.'

Isabel tied the strings of her bonnet beneath her chin. 'Title-digger? What title is Mrs

Greenwood expecting to excavate? The Colonel's wife?'

'When he inherits from his grandfather he becomes an earl and the old chap is in his eighties.' After a pause Rachel said, 'I think Colonel Hauke seems particularly taken with you. Every evening you chat together or play chess. Has he been flirting with you?'

'No. We just find things to talk about.' At Rachel's arch look, Isabel laughingly elaborated. 'For instance, that first night we started talking because he wanted to apologise for his mother's inquisitiveness about Marcus and my husband.'

'That *was* a little indecorous. But I'm sure there was no malice in it. Had I imagined she might press you about…that I would not have asked her here.'

'No harm was done.'

'It always looks as though he is flirting with you,' Rachel persisted. 'When you are together he seems quite…intense.'

Isabel simply smiled neutrally. He hadn't flirted with her last night, or any night, but he had this morning…most definitely. And she had flirted back, even knowing he was a man with a fiancée in the wings and no proper interest in her. And that should worry her. But it didn't. For the first time since she had been with Marcus's father, she'd enjoyed and responded to a man's attention, however lightly given, however insincere.

But she'd been propositioned recently. Not that she expected Colonel Hauke to present her with anything so explicitly vulgar as his protection. He was the Earl of Devane's friend; Connor was married to her sister. A liaison between them would be in extreme bad taste. And, she thought on an inner smile to lift her spirits, she couldn't credit her own conceit. She had not yet known the man for one whole week. All the Colonel had done was flirt with her for a little while and she was girding herself to rebuff his advances. But then, should they come...*would* she rebuff them?

Chapter Four

Isabel was softly humming, tipping her purchases out of her basket onto the bed when Noreen tapped at her door. At the instruction to enter the servant did so and handed Isabel a note.

'It's from Mrs Hauke, ma'am.' The explanation was rushed and the Irish woman seemed keen to absent herself.

'Noreen?'

A few reluctant steps brought the flush-faced servant once more over the threshold.

'Marcus is not in his room or in the nursery. Is he studying in the library?'

'Ah…I think he's…umm…he's most likely after being in the stables with Sam,' Noreen mumbled. 'I saw him heading that way.'

'Did Marcus say how he did at school today?'

Noreen's freckles were concealed by fierce floridity. 'No, ma'am. But the Father did say a sermon when I arrived to fetch him home. I was going to tell you in a while…after you'd had time to catch breath.' Noreen's pale blue eyes slanted at Isabel's bonnet still atop her thick fawn hair. 'That little devil Michael Murphy is a bad sort is what I'm thinking, begging your pardon for boldly saying so, ma'am. But after that day when he took your son away to town in that bad weather, and me nearly mad and tearing out me hair with wondering where he'd got to… The Father says the two of them were down by the wharf this afternoon, fishing. Young master 'ud be best off keeping his distance from that Murphy boy. Himself is sure to be coming over to see you about it all.'

Isabel looked at the note in her hand. 'Thank you, Noreen,' was all she said as she dismissed the servant. She closed her eyes and sank her small teeth painfully into her lower lip. Noreen had just let her know in no uncertain terms that she thought her son was lacking elementary discipline and she was lacking in parental duty.

Disciplining Marcus by sending him to his room was no use. When she had locked him in he had escaped via his bedroom window, risking serious injury in the process. She didn't ever seriously contemplate corporal punishment or banishing him to bed without his dinner. She couldn't bear the thought of him hurt or hungry.

She picked up the bag of candies she'd chosen for him, folded the top over, imprisoning the treats, and put the bag in a drawer. She had enjoyed her day. She had even forgotten about Colonel Hauke for a while, although she couldn't fathom why the wretched man should so dominate her thoughts on such short acquaintance.

With a sigh Isabel looked at the note still clasped in her hand and broke the wafer. Claudine's neatly scripted message politely requested a remedy for her headache, if it was not too much of an imposition, for the pain was still plaguing her.

Isabel had the necessary ingredients to hand. Going to a cupboard, she extracted some dark glass jars and took a little from each. Lavender, willow bark and vervain were each carefully measured. Folding the grainy powder into scraps of paper, Isabel thrust those into her skirt pocket. She was about to quit the room when she remembered her bonnet still tied beneath her chin. With a dispirited sigh she removed it, tossing it on to the bed before she closed the door and made for the East Wing.

Claudine answered her light tap within a moment, then went to flop back on her bed. Isabel looked at her with a worried frown. Quickly she dropped to her knees and chafed Claudine's cold hands. 'Has the pain worsened since this morning?'

Claudine nodded, keeping her eyes lowered, then abruptly stood up. 'No. It is something else. I have a pain, but I think it is squeezing my heart rather than my head. This is so awkward for me. I do not know where to begin. We barely know each other, yet I must speak to you of a very personal thing and I know now you do not like to talk of your bereavement. Perhaps if I show you something… Oh, I don't know,' she suddenly cried and her small hands cupped her face. 'You will think me a fool if what I suspect is wrong. *C'est incroyable!*' She again sank to the bed.

Isabel bent close to Claudine, shocked by the woman's very real distress. Her elegant chignon had loosened and strands of silvered hair were trailing her wan cheeks. The hands concealing her face were all a-tremble too. 'I think now you must explain what ails you.' At Claudine's mournful look, glistening up between tear-spiky lashes, Isabel smiled encouragingly.

Claudine pulled close an ornate walnut box and lifted the lid. Within reposed a neat sewing set. Coloured threads and small scissors and needles were ranged neatly. Isabel saw, too, a gilt-framed miniature nestling on the silks. Claudine gently, reverently lifted out the painting and proffered it.

The portrait was of a solemn-faced child, blond and beautiful; the likeness to Isabel's son was remarkable. She smiled at Claudine. 'You are right, Mrs Hauke. One of your grandchildren is the image of Marcus. This then must be...Phillipe. The grave expression he wears! So like Marcus in a mood.'

'That is not Phillipe...or Sophie. It is Etienne's portrait, painted over twenty-five years ago. He was about six years old.'

The information caused Isabel to freeze. It was a long, long time since she'd heard that name, but it never would quit that secret corner of her mind and still had the power to wound her.

'Etienne?' she queried in a whisper.

'Etienne...my son. He sometimes calls himself Steven, merely to annoy me, I think, for he knew I preferred the French version of his name. Even when he was little he would do all in his power to vex me.'

'Colonel Hauke? His name is Etienne?' Isabel forced out from a mouth so dry her tongue seemed welded to her palate. Stop being so dull! she told herself crossly. Etienne is a very common French name. Colonel Hauke has French blood. Why should that matter to me? Yet her mind clung to the news, absorbed it, refused to surrender it.

Struggling to display calm and reason, she said, 'There certainly is a likeness to Marcus. But fair children seem similar, don't you think? The features are so tiny it is hard to discern any important little differences—'

'I must tell you something,' Claudine cut into Isabel's calm reasoning. 'You can think I am being *stupide,* you can tell me to mind my own business, but I have been worrying so since I came back earlier. I had caught my gown on a bramble and was going to mend it,' she obliquely explained her seeking the sewing box. 'I found this picture beneath the green silks. Yesterday I could not even tell you where I had left this or when I last looked upon it.' A faint smile preceded, 'I am not one for doing the mending. Marie does such tasks. But today my maid is gone to market and not yet back so I decided to… Oh, it doesn't matter about that! It is fate that I should find it today of all days. The very same day I meet your Marcus.'

'I don't understand.' Isabel murmured, her heart hammering.

Claudine sat down, with a weary sigh, on the bed. 'First I must tell you a little of our history. My late husband, Etienne's father, and I…we did not have a happy marriage. It was simply a convenient arrangement: I was in

England, visiting a school friend, when the Bastille was stormed. I was just eighteen, the daughter of a French count and I could not return home for fear of being incarcerated with the rest of my family. I needed proper protection and Benjamin, for his own reasons, needed a wife to please his father. So we married without any love, just a little respect and desperation.'

Claudine smiled sadly then said, 'Of course things rarely improve in such circumstances. It was wrong but inevitable that we would both soon seek comfort elsewhere. I was unfaithful first I'm ashamed to say. Benjamin also found someone to love. Mrs Smith was a young widow...or so she claimed. I think she was a professional courtesan who had never been near a church. She had a child by Benjamin, a boy, just a year after Etienne was born legitimately of our union. A mutual friend once told me that the bastard son and the legitimate son were so alike they might have been twins. By the time Etienne was thirteen he was my boy...dark-haired and quite French in looks. I heard that Mrs Smith's son stayed blond into adulthood. I have to know, please forgive me for asking, but I cannot get it from my mind that you might have married my husband's illegitimate son. Was your husband's name Christopher? You said he was a soldier. Christopher joined the army. When my husband refused to divorce me and marry her Mrs Smith moved far away, close to York, I learned, and married a man there. His name might have been Forrester.'

Isabel was numb with shock. She had listened intently, yet felt that she had missed vital information. Slowly she focused on Claudine and said, 'No, my son's father was not called Christopher. I hope that puts your mind at rest.'

Claudine visibly relaxed. 'I'm so sorry to have bothered you with it all.' A sheepish look accompanied the apology. 'But the portrait, the likeness, your sister told me you lived in York...it is all quite a rare and strange coincidence, is it not?'

Isabel forced a smile through stiff lips. 'Yes; quite an odd coincidence.' Her mind felt in turmoil, yet somehow she remembered the powder and extracted it from her pocket. 'I'll fetch some hot water to mix this and make you a brew.'

Claudine brightened. 'I think I might not need it after all. I feel better now I have got that off my chest.' A light sigh stressed her relief. 'Your sister tells me she has arranged an impromptu dinner party. Vincent and his daughters are to dine here tonight and some other people...the Fitzgeralds. They are the people you like, *non?*' Humming, she went to the closet and opened it, head tilted in consideration of the gowns within.

Isabel barely noticed the dresses pulled out for her to view; her eyes were once again with the small portrait. She picked it up and asked hoarsely, 'May I borrow this, Mrs Hauke? I think some people might like to see it. I will return it soon.'

'*Bien sûr!* And, please, no more Mrs Hauke. Now we have talked so intimately I think we are friends, *non?*' Claudine twirled about with a damson silk gown held against her slender body. Her pencilled eyebrows shot up questioningly.

'It's lovely.' The bright compliment flowed in her wake as Isabel quit the room.

* * *

Dusk was falling; what light remained was nebulous and deceiving, but adequate for her to know the likeness was true.

Isabel was standing by the window in her bedroom. Obsessively she once more turned the miniature to face the glass to absorb the twilight. She stared at each tiny feature in turn until not only were they imprinted on her agitated mind, but so too was every faint flake and fissure in the painted canvas. Her heart was thudding a slow tattoo beneath her ribs when finally she lay the portrait on her bed. Still she could not let go of it and as she circled back and forth between her clothes press, the chest of drawers and the washstand, her eyes were invariably locked with two brown dots that gleamed between black fringes. They seemed to follow her, mock her. She would never have guessed it to be Etienne Hauke's portrait. The man looked nothing like his child's self. Had she once met Christopher, his half-brother? Would he have masqueraded as Etienne? If so, why?

She washed automatically and was towelling her face when Noreen knocked at her door. The maid seemed in better spirits than when Isabel had spoken to her earlier. 'Faith! You're in the dark, ma'am.' Immediately Noreen went about, lighting tapers and lamps. The heavy curtains were closed against the residue of daylight.

On learning from the maid that Marcus was fed, bathed and in his nightclothes, Isabel felt a pang of guilt that since returning from Claudine's room she had barely given a thought to her own flesh and blood. Her whole attention was focused on the lifeless impostor on her bed. She sat at her mirror, allowed Noreen to dress her hair then help her step into her newest gown. It was cream muslin sprigged with apricot rosebuds. She knew it was stylish and suited her colouring, but how she looked seemed unimportant tonight. The appearance of the visage in the portrait dominated her thoughts.

Noreen chattered to her about this evening's little party, informing her in her broad Irish brogue that the Ormondes had already arrived an hour too early, sending Miss Rachel into a spin. Isabel was barely listening. As her hair was brushed in soothing strokes she relaxed. Perhaps she had been affected by Claudine's hysteria. Perhaps what was needed was a more objective opinion on the portrait. Abruptly she said, 'What do you think of the little picture on my bed, Noreen?'

Noreen looked a trifle surprised, poised as she was to defeat some rebellious curls. She put down the silver-backed brush and did as she was bid.

'Mother Mary! Now isn't that the look he wears?' Noreen grimaced in a fair approximation of the expression she was scrutinising. 'Sure an' I'm amazed you got Master Marcus to stay still long enough for it to be painted. He's a fine-looking lad, so he is. A rogue of a heart-breaker in the making, is what I'm thinking!' Reverently the picture was returned to the bed. 'Was it done in York?'

Isabel got up from her stool and retrieved the miniature from the quilt. 'No,' was all she said on a dismissing smile, as unconsciously she moved to a lighted candle and allowed its flame to illuminate the fair face so she could again study it.

Rachel looked about at her assembled guests. 'The Misses Ormonde seem much taken with the Colonel,' she remarked to her sister. 'But then who can blame them? As you know I am quite partial to him myself. We all had a good ride towards the village this morning. Claudine has a fine seat: she again outstripped me quite easily over the fences. You should have come along, if for no other reason than to uphold the Merediths' family pride.'

Isabel simply smiled at the compliment to her riding ability. But her eyes did settle on the Colonel...Etienne, she changed it to in her mind. The Ormonde girls had, indeed, cornered him and seemed to be enjoying an animated discussion with him. Isabel intended much the same for Etienne Hauke. She imagined he would prefer the dialogue with the young ladies presently entrapping him.

'You look pale. Are you cold or ailing?' Rachel asked her sombrely quiet sister.

Isabel treated Rachel to a smile. 'No, I'm just a little preoccupied. Marcus is again in trouble with his lessons. I see that Clodagh and Liam have just arrived.'

'Are you not hungry?'

The abrupt question startled Isabel from a

dark reflection. 'Yes...no...not really.' She laid down the fork that had idly been pushing food about her plate.

'You seem...nervous. I hope it's not my presence ruining your appetite.'

'Not at all,' Isabel returned lightly. 'I'm afraid I overindulged in town today. We... Clodagh, Liam and I...enjoyed a very fine tea at the Fiddle and Flute.'

'That's a shame...I wish I'd known,' Etienne Hauke said.

Isabel slanted him a look. 'Are you rueing my poor appetite?'

'No, I'm regretting not knowing you would be stopping at the Fiddle and Flute. You could have brought back my trunk. Apparently it was there earlier today, having been returned by the innkeeper of the Black Swan who managed to repossess it from a couple of felons who had purloined it from the coach bringing it here. I am again kitted out courtesy of Connor's wardrobe.'

Isabel's eyes drifted to an immaculate cambric cuff adorning the negligent dark hand reposing on the table. It was difficult detaching her eyes from long fingers toying with silver.

An opportunity had presented itself to casually chat, and the other guests were all occupied. Just an innocent enquiry to start... 'When Connor and Rachel were engaged years ago, were you invited to the wedding, Colonel Hauke?'

His lips twitched ruefully. 'I was. Flinte couldn't be sure that his stepbrother, Jason Davenport, would survive his stag party. I was appointed stand-by groomsman. Jason is a serious imbiber, you see. In the event, of course, it was Connor who nearly didn't survive his stag night...'

Isabel was aware of a sombre note honing his tone and the way his eyes flickered low and oblique to target her sister.

'So you were in England at that time rather than abroad on military duties.'

'I was here for several weeks; longer than I intended to stay. It was a terrible time for Connor.'

'Yes, it was. But eventually it turned right for them.' Isabel grittily championed her sister.

'Who would have thought it?' he bluntly countered.

'You stayed with Connor in London, at that time?'

She was aware of a more probing look searing the side of her face. Her interrogation was losing subtlety.

'If my memory serves me, I stayed in London with Connor for a while and visited my grandparents in Cambridge. My grandfather has a habit of sending urgent and vital messages summoning me to his bedside because he is sure he is about to die. It is all just a ploy to make me visit. He thinks I am not quite the dutiful heir I ought to be. He keeps threatening to cut me off without a brass farthing of his.'

The humour in his voice made Isabel relax a little. So did the information that his time had been spent at those locations. 'It's fortunate you have ample brass farthings of your own, sir. An inheritance is not usually a matter for banter.'

Etienne laughed and looked at her. 'Have my bachelor prospects been under discussion?' he asked softly.

'I shouldn't have said that. I don't know why I did.'

'Don't concern yourself, Mrs Forrester. I'm enough of a realist to know that ladies discuss the financial status of bachelors. A decade ago, when my mother was hawking my sister, Monique, about in the marriage mart, there was talk of little else in our household than gentlemen's fortunes and prospects. I could tell you now how much Roddy Beauchamp or Tim Pendergast had in the bank ten years ago.'

Isabel blushed at the arrant cynicism in his tone. Hastily she picked up the threads of their previous conversation. 'So your grandfather sent a message to London threatening dire consequences if you didn't visit him?'

Etienne grunted a laugh. 'He did. And I remember feeling quite amazed that it ever reached me at all. It had been directed to Mayfair, then rerouted to the north. It was delivered just a day later to my lodgings in York.'

Chapter Five

'Y... York?'

The word was expelled on a strangled gasp. Etienne pushed back in his chair and took a scrutinising glance at her, guessing that embarrassment was causing her to stutter. Isabel Forrester had hitherto seemed coolly composed.

After many years, barely giving it a thought, tendrils of intelligence about Rachel's jilting of Connor seemed to be constantly infiltrating his mind. Of the four Meredith girls, one sister had accompanied the runaway bride to York to stay with an aunt. Logically it would be this sister. Isabel Forrester and Rachel Flinte seemed of a similar age. They were obviously close friends as well as kin to be living under the same roof. Again he pondered why Edgar Meredith wasn't providing a roof over the heads of his widowed daughter and his grandson. It seemed increasingly likely her husband had left her wanting.

'It was a long while ago, but I remember travelling to York and staying for a couple of days.' Mentally he grimaced at the memory. Quite an absurd task he had set himself too, haring, fired with moral outrage, after the fugitive Miss who had brought his friend so low he had nearly died. Connor's stepbrother, Jason, had found the heartbroken bridegroom in a drunken stupor on Clapham Common. Had he not, Connor would most certainly have died from exposure that freezing night.

Isabel couldn't trust herself to look at him. Her stomach was in knots, her heart drumming slowly, deafening her. She could no longer ignore what that seemingly inconsequential snippet of information might mean. Too many colliding coincidences were slotting snugly together. A kaleidoscope of images was jumbling in her mind, but she was frightened to demand he see it too. Yet she would not be able to live with her conscience if she did nothing, acted the coward, and allowed him to leave Ireland without talking to him further.

She needed just one more answer, a final piece of proof to tip the balance. Persisting with her investigation here...now...in company, wasn't fitting. But she must persist. She owed that much to Marcus.

'Might I have a private word with you later? There is something I think we ought talk about...concerning that time...' eventually was forced through her chill, stiff lips.

'Of course.' He smiled at a profile now obscured. Her head had dipped towards her plate and spirals of caramel-coloured hair curtained her cheek. Was she about to admit that she had been in York in the company of the renegade bride? She seemed loyal to Rachel, as a sister should be. If she had guessed his reason for travelling there had been to meddle in something that had been outside his role, perhaps she was not so much embarrassed as indignant on her sister's behalf and was about to reprimand him. He mused with masculine interest on a reprimand from Mrs Forrester and decided he would find it no hardship.

Although the dining room was humming with lively conversation, a still silence whispered between them. When Isabel gave no venue for their post-prandial tête à tète, Etienne eventually suggested lightly, 'Here? The drawing room? An assignation in the summer house?' A sideways glance indicated double doors that opened on to a vast stone terrace milk-bathed in moonlight.

His teasing tone made Isabel's head snap up. He was laughing at her, she realised furiously. He found her gravity amusing. A feral green glance raked his face and with an amount of triumph she noticed his mockery fade to a frown. 'The library is a private place to meet. It is situated by the foot of the stairs,' she informed him coolly. Soon he might be laughing on the other side of his face, she realised with some satisfaction.

'Yes...I know where it is.'

She ignored the wry comment. There was still a time to arrange. 'When we are finished dinner, I shall leave first; perhaps after ten minutes you would join me there.'

'I'd be delighted,' he drawled, but his nonchalance wasn't totally convincing. 'It sounds very clandestine. I'm intrigued. Am I to be told something shocking?'

Isabel couldn't prevent a breath of bitter laughter almost choking her. Her gaze flashed again to his, locked on to earthy dots glittering through sooty lashes. Their lifeless like had recently been tracking her from a portrait. 'Indeed, sir, I think you ought to prepare yourself to be shocked.' It was delivered so quietly he had to incline his dark head to catch the words.

'Wake up, dear...'

Marcus rolled over, irritably kicked his legs about in voluminous cotton, before burrowing his small skull comfortably into his feather pillow with a thumb parting his teeth.

'No, you must wake up, my love!' Isabel attempted to quieten the agitation in her voice so as not to startle him. 'You may come downstairs for a little while,' she cajoled. 'Mrs Dooley has bilberry jam tarts cooling on a rack.' The enticement was augmented with a soft finger stroking at his cheek.

Sleepy as he was, nevertheless his intelligent little mind sought ulterior motives. 'I've done my sums...Noreen made me. Don't want to go back downstairs.' Marcus declined his mother's generosity and again nestled into his warm cocoon.

'No sums…or verbs…I promise. Come, you may take your soldiers and set them out in the kitchen. There is someone…one of the guests…I would like you to meet later. Have you seen Colonel Hauke who is staying here, Marcus?'

Marcus shook his drowsy head against the pillow as his legs emerged from his nightshirt and poked over the side of the bed. Jam tarts and soldiers were very tempting. He allowed his mother to help him into his dressing gown and slippers.

Mrs Dooley had been happy enough to give Marcus a plate of tarts and a draught-free corner by the cooking range for his army to mass in. Before quitting the kitchens, Isabel had given the senior scullion, a sweet girl of about fourteen, called Betty, an instruction on when to bring Marcus to the library. Isabel, her fists preventing sprigged muslin from impeding her feet, then raced down the winding corridor towards the library. Halfway to her destination, her silent flight over the runners faltered with her courage. She stumbled into a window alcove, rested her hot brow against cold glass. Her heart was battering so hard at her ribs they ached. She was wrong; it was nonsense. Such scandals were fiction! They did not really happen! But then scandalous nonsense had been her whole life for eight years. She wanted to know. There was just that one more discovery to make. With a shivery restorative breath she sedately walked on and entered the library with a composed smile.

He was already there, lounging back at his ease in a chair. He looked as though he didn't have a care in the world. He immediately stood as she entered and the hand cradling a book across its broad palm snapped closed. The tome was placed on a table. 'I was beginning to think I might have got the wrong library. Is there another?'

'No. I'm sorry. I was delayed. I had to see to my son.' The words were truthful and concise. Her smile remained intact.

He smiled too; his eyes watched her.

She walked closer, her expression neutral. Limpid green eyes scanned his face, searching, seeking a hint of something solid. But in her mind all was spectral…just shapes and shadows. Her memory for noise was sharper and rustled up moaning wind and leaves sighing beneath driving rain. But there was only one sure way to know. Could she just reach out and touch…

He was watching her with narrowed eyes, faint amusement lifting a corner of his mouth. He was not displeased. She sensed his growing anticipation. With a flash of insight she understood what he read into the situation. He thought she had lured him here to solicit his protection. Over dinner she had stupidly hinted she knew he was wealthy. He had been cynically amused to know she had made it her business to find out. A hint of a sneer had coarsened his cultured voice when he admitted he knew women gossiped over gentlemen's wealth and prospects. After a few days of nothing more than civility between them, this morning they had flirted a little. She had refused his offer to ride out with him…but coyly. She cringed at a truth she couldn't deny. Soon he was due to leave for England. He thought she was done with playing hard to get and wanted to hook him before he left. The arrogance of the man! Just because she was a lone woman with a child, he expected... The scorn withered in her throat. It wasn't outlandish. She understood why he might think that. Her situation made her vulnerable prey to lechers. After Aunt Florence died and she and Marcus were living alone and frugally in York, a local businessman had sent her a detailed offer, delivered by a leering manservant. She had been shocked, not so much by his presumption, but by knowing he had noticed her that way. Previously he had barely acknowledged her existence other than to nod and mumble at her every Sunday morning at service.

'At dinner we were talking of York and how I came to be there all those years ago.' It was a gentle prompting.

Isabel's small white teeth were bared briefly in an approximation of a smile. 'Indeed we were. What did you think of York?'

'A plaguey place.'

The fierce look she sent him elicited a better explanation than that brusque complaint.

'I chose the wrong time to visit such a fine city. As I arrived York was suffering a scarletina epidemic. That was one reason I didn't linger there, but travelled on to Cambridge to see my grandparents before I returned overseas.'

'You had no reason to linger in York?' His words echoed back at him, sounding inconsequential. *He'd no reason to linger in York,* circled her mind woundingly.

'None whatsoever. To be truthful, I wish I'd never gone to the infernal place. I made a mistake. Hindsight can be a most humbling thing.'

'I see.'

After a brief pause heavy with tension Etienne stated, 'When Rachel jilted Connor and absconded she went to York accompanied by one of her sisters. It was you.'

'Yes, it was me.'

'You were safe from the infection?'

'From the scarletina… Yes.'

'Did you stay there long?'

'Yes. I was there a long time. Until quite recently.' She was aware of his intelligent gaze on her. Of course he sensed an undercurrent to the stilted phrases batting back and forth between them. With an inspiriting breath she walked closer, looked up into his face with eyes as arctic as the ocean.

'Have I offended you in some way, Mrs Forrester?' he asked quietly.

'Indeed, I believe you might have, sir, and if you would answer me one simple but, I regret, personal question I shall know for certain and can then opt to make either accusations or apologies.'

Etienne spread his hands in a gesture that parted his immaculate jacket, displaying an expanse of solid muscular torso adorned in slub silk. 'Ask away, madam, by all means.'

The words were polite and silky with mockery. Perhaps he deemed it all unnecessarily histrionic. The drama was real—so real that she itched to smack the self-assurance from his face. Her hands were gripped behind her back, fingers entwined. Be patient! she admonished herself. His smugness won't last a tongue-lashing. And so much more dignified than striking out. 'Do you have a long scar on the right side of your skull from a wound inflicted about eight years ago by a French sword?'

Her answer was clear, signalled by an instinctive suspicion narrowing his eyes. At the first glimpse of his guilt, she felt winded as though she had received a blow to the stomach. In a voice that trembled with her own astonishment and disbelief she exacted more final proof. 'And when you were in York, were you thin…much thinner than you are now, because you had been a prisoner of war for many months? And had your hair been cropped very short to enable the surgeon to attend that head wound you received whilst escaping? And, at the risk of sounding melodramatic, on one dark and stormy night did you meet a young woman in woodland and reveal that much of your history? Did you inform her your name was Etienne and you held the rank of Captain in the Hussars? And would you like me to tell you now how I could possibly know all of that?' By the time she finished her voice was vibrating with emotion.

'Please do.'

It was the sum of his response, but those two words were bitten out with such a menacing softness that they stopped her heart. For a moment Isabel could do no more than swallow convulsively and fret that her final proof—every bit of it—was not quite conclusive enough. But of course it was; she had seen each vital fact truthfully register with him.

There was no going back. Courageously she began. 'I too, must admit to being put out by that epidemic of scarletina. Tonight I've learned that pestilence has a human form. You. You say you had no reason to linger in York so I doubt our...encounter...made much of an impression on you eight years ago. I suspect you would not be able to recall a lot of it now. Let me jog your memory. Yes, I accompanied Rachel when she jilted Connor and fled to York. Within a few days of our arrival the infection was running out of control. One evening when Rachel and Aunt Florence were abed I went to Elm Wood to gather ingredients for a concoction to strengthen our constitutions against the disease. Of necessity I ventured there at night because Aunt Florence would not let either Rachel or me out of the house during the day. She was terrified one of us would succumb to the infection and blame for it would fall on her. So when I should have been safe in my bedchamber, I was not. Had the night not turned unexpectedly stormy I might have heard and seen you coming, but with the moon lost and thunder crashing—'

'What are you saying?' he snapped in a voice more alarming for its icy restraint. 'That I raped you?'

Isabel's complexion drained of blood. 'No...' she whispered.

'No, indeed, madam.' His voice was low, silky with steel. 'I might have been guilty that night, but not of forcing myself on an unwilling woman. Now you have refreshed my memory, I can recall the incident, and pleasurable it was too, for us both. The most vivid impression I have of that coupling is a woman clinging to me, begging me not to leave her...to come again, if you will. And I'm amazed to learn I had the time or stamina to pass on so much information about myself. Conversation seemed to be the last thing on your mind.'

Isabel physically flinched as though slapped. 'None of those first sordid details matter now,' she whispered hoarsely.

'I beg to differ on that score. It's obvious you've brought me here to accuse me of abusing you. To me, those first sordid details matter very much. I'm not even sure I was the seducer.'

'I don't know how you dare say that! But
then you're certainly no gentleman, are you,
sir?' Isabel felt tears of utter mortification sting
her eyes. She blinked them away, rallying
every atom of courage she possessed not to
flee. From being moments ago ignorant of her
existence eight years ago, how easily he now
could reminisce on what she would sooner
they both forgot. 'This is all that matters now,'
she blurted. Shaking hands extracted the miniature from her pocket and dropped it down on
the table. 'Your mother first showed me this
portrait this afternoon. She says it is your likeness, painted when you were about six years
old.'

Etienne flicked a glance at it. His eyes were
arrested, narrowing on a pale oval with a sense
of foreboding. He remembered the portrait
vaguely. He recalled thinking last time he saw
it—God only knew when that had been—that
it was hard to believe he once had been so fair.
Recently he had seen a face like that. He had
seen an Irish child and thought he looked familiar. Images tumbled into his brain: a handsome boy beneath his stallion's hooves, a win-
try day sullen with sleet; an Irish woman

swaddled against the elements glaring at him as, muttering and cursing in a broad brogue, she hauled the little scapegrace away to safety. Grave uneasiness was turning in the pit of his stomach. He recalled speaking to the lad and something about their brief exchange had jarred on his mind. Now he knew what it was. The child had spoken with an English accent.

That chilling reflection was being submerged by more sultry memories. Thoughts of warm, silken skin, sleek with rain, and a wanton maid who gave freely and spoke little rolled through his mind. This, then, was the earthy nymph he'd tumbled in a gamekeeper's hide! It was unbelievable! Damnation! Had he only known just how gently bred she was he would have put her on her feet and mounted his horse instead. He'd learned the hard way she was a virgin who spoke with the accent of a gentlewoman. God only knew he could have been forgiven for mistaking her for a practised harlot. He had recalled feeling sceptical that an ingenue would allow him to help her dress. Yet she had. He could picture them giggling together like children as he clumsily tied the bows on her chemise and fought with her petticoats. They had huddled close together beneath his caped coat until the worst of the downpour passed, whispering a few words in between kisses and cringes as thunder crashed and rain lashed the shelter. She had volunteered little about herself and had seemed as keen as he to go once their passion was sated. But before she'd raced off under dripping branches she had soothed his guilt with more kisses, murmured reassurances that she was well and happy, before begging him to meet her there again tomorrow. He'd agreed, from bogus chivalry, knowing full well that tomorrow he would be halfway to Ashcombe House in Cambridge to see if, this time, his grandfather really was about to expire. The same empty courtesy had made him offer more than once to escort her to her lodgings. Her adamant refusal had been a boon.

As he'd galloped through storm-soaked countryside he had obsessively thought of her and her frantic ardour. By the time he reached the Cambridge borders he had convinced himself he wasn't to blame. Only a *demi-vierge,* a woman versed in the arts of love if technically still intact, could have responded in the way she did. She spoke cultured English, but then so did plenty of courtesans schooled by rich old men who paid for companionship as well as sexual release. By the time he'd reached Ashcombe House he had persuaded himself it was best to forget her and was concentrating on someone he could trust: Lady Avery. At twenty-four it would not have occurred to him to have felt guilty over deceiving his mistress with a casual liaison, even though at the time he was besotted with the newly widowed baroness.

The rap at the door made Isabel jump. Swiftly she went to open it, silently praising young Betty for being a few minutes late, yet, so fortuitously, just on time. With a dismissing nod for the young scullion, Isabel drew her son into the room.

'Etienne!' Marcus exclaimed excitedly and, wriggling his fingers free of his mother's, he hurtled across the room, almost tripping as his dressing gown hampered his busy little legs.

'How does he know your name?' The demand was explosive.

'Would you mind explaining just what is going on now?' Etienne blasted at the same time, glaring back with tight-lipped ferocity. His thin mouth was bracketed by livid white grooves.

'Etienne nearly knocked me down,' Marcus happily added to the jumble of dialogue, making the two adults present unlock their combatant glares and stare at him instead.

Isabel felt maternal rage flare in her. She flashed a look of pure aggression at Etienne at her son's words. 'You nearly knocked him down?' Her voice hummed a low note of threat.

'It was when Murphy and me went to town and the Father found out and got Noreen to fetch me home. I ran away to warn Murphy that the Father was after us and Etienne nearly pulped me with Storm. He's high and black and shiny. He's better even than Uncle Connor's Pharaoh,' he proclaimed, naming the finest mount in the Earl of Devane's stable.

Etienne couldn't detach his eyes from Marcus. He was staring at the boy, ashen-faced, as though he was a harbinger of vile calamity. Isabel realised that was exactly how he would view her precious son. He would be a ghastly nuisance, and better left concealed in shadows. But she and Marcus had remained out of sight, unacknowledged for too long. She didn't want or need this man. For days past she had thought him attractive, had thought if only... Now she knew why he held such allure. Subconsciously she had recognised that once he had meant everything to her. On occasions too numerous to count she had slipped away to keep a vigil in Elm Wood. Now she finally knew just what a fool she had been. Here was her chivalrous hero, the man she was sure must have met disaster or death to prevent him returning to claim her. Here he stood in all his healthy arrogance. For weeks, months, a year she had dreamed of him; had trusted his promise to return. Now she knew he had forgotten her as soon as he had ridden out of the trees. Even with a babe in arms, it was a few months more before she had finally discarded her precious memories as ashes. She didn't want him, this callous philanderer. She had survived without him for eight hard years. But never once had she relinquished hope of respectability for Marcus. Unbelievably, through a pall of scandal and misery, she was watching her son's future emerge. Her instinct was to reach out and snatch and never cede, no matter what this man threatened.

Etienne glanced from Marcus to Isabel. The skin on his face was tight and white as parchment and huge-pupilled brown eyes gleamed like hellish embers. 'This is your son?'

'Did you nearly knock him down?' she countered.

'He ran in front of my horse to get his hat. He was unhurt.'

'I did run in front of his horse,' Marcus chirpily endorsed. 'Etienne told me off and said he could have easily pulped me. I asked him his name and he said I should remember my manners and say, what is your name, *sir.*'

Etienne spoke next, in a voice made husky and stilted with rage. 'I see your point. You've displayed the goods long enough, madam. I've no intention of bartering in his presence. Have the boy returned to his bed. There are obviously vital things we need to discuss.'

The cold disgust in his tone squeezed at Isabel's heart. He thought her capable of exploiting her beloved son for coinage! Her chin shot up at his autocratic tone. But the edict was sensible. Indeed, there were vital things for them to discuss and she didn't want her son witnessing more of the belligerence between them that was breeding fast as disease.

Before she could ring for a servant to take her son back upstairs, a knock came on the door. Noreen Smith nervously appeared and loitered on the threshold. Behind her tiny figure loomed a giant of a man garbed all in black. Isabel recognised the visitor at once and her heart plummeted to her toes. Father Maguire had, as Noreen prophesied, come over and was no doubt ready to repeat his sermon.

Noreen's pale blue eyes swivelled between the master's friend and the mistress's sister. The Colonel's expression looked dark as thunder. Mrs Forrester looked white as a shroud. 'Beg pardon, ma'am,' she blurted on a nervous frown. 'Father Maguire is here.' A speaking look lingered on Isabel. She might just as well have said, 'Don't blame me! I told you he was coming.'

Isabel felt hysteria hacking at the back of her throat. There could hardly have been a less opportune time for the priest to arrive.

'Good evening to you, Mrs Forrester.' Father Maguire slipped past Noreen with surprising ease, considering his stature. His black trilby was not on his pewter hair, but stuck under an arm. A nod acknowledged Etienne Hauke. 'It's sorry I am to be interrupting, but it's important I speak to you about your son. Sure and something must be done!' Down the considerable length of a hooked nose, just one of the priest's eyes narrowed on Marcus. Silently, swiftly, the boy sidled to his mother's side.

'Have you been a good honest boy and told your mother what devilry you've been about today?' It was a voice laden with reprisal. 'Now don't look so surprised, Marcus Forrester, didn't I warn you what it is I must do?' A look slew to Isabel. 'He's in need of a thrashing, Mrs Forrester, if ever he is to learn and be a credit to you and himself. And what a sin if he's not mending his ways for he'll never be a credit to his father's memory either, God rest him.'

'I will be! My father was a brave soldier.'

'Hush, Marcus!' Isabel croaked, a hand stroking at his flushed cheek, silencing him. She closed her eyes, imperceptibly. Then a composed voice she barely recognised as hers said, 'Father Maguire, I will speak to you to-morrow. I am aware there has been a problem…another problem…but I…it is not now convenient.'

'Another problem? Hah!' the priest spat out. 'Too many problems, Mrs Forrester! If you will not let me discipline this boy then he must be taken out of school. He is a bad influence on the boys who either do as they must or take their punishment. I know it is hard for you being a widow as you are. Shall I be speaking to his uncle? What the boy needs, to be sure, is a firm hand. Shall I be speaking to the Earl of Devane about it all?'

'No. You may speak to me.'

Chapter Six

'Who are you then, sir? A relative?'

'I'm Etienne Hauke, a friend and army colleague of the Earl of Devane. I'm pleased to meet you.' The two men shook hands.

Isabel felt her son's small fingers slip against hers. She squeezed loving reassurance against his plucking while discreetly observing the adult males present. Both seemed different. Father Maguire was wearing a look of deliverance that had ironed the pleats from his lofty brow. Isabel respected him as a good, hard-working man who would always strive to do his duty. If, in the process, he upset her, she knew it wouldn't bother him too much. But he was chary of alienating her brother-in-law, who was a most influential man in Ireland. He seemed confident a fitting compromise would be reached now an intermediary, in the imposing form of a comrade of the Earl's, had stepped in to rescue the situation.

As for Etienne, the ogre and his anger were gone. Suave Colonel Hauke was back. If his charming smile was a little tight, Father Maguire didn't seem to notice. If a hard handshake was crushing the bones in the cleric's fingers, he piously suffered in silence. Neither did he seem to object to the affable hand on his shoulder deftly steering him away into the hall.

Isabel watched them talking together for a moment before she rallied her sense enough to instruct a gawping Noreen to take Marcus to his bed. 'Tomorrow we must talk about all this, Marcus. Father Maguire is right when he says that no more mischief will be tolerated,' she softly warned him.

He bowed his small head so his chin touched his chest. Chastened, he allowed Noreen to lead him away. As her downcast son was quitting the room, her radiant sister was entering, with small crab-like steps, so she could survey the people dotted about her hallway.

'We were wondering where on earth you had got to, Isabel!' Rachel declared without once looking at her sister. Her curious blue eyes were flitting between her nephew, climbing the stairs with Noreen in attendance, and the gentlemen deep in discussion.

'Father Maguire chose a rather inopportune moment to arrive on...a mission,' Isabel told her sister a trifle breathlessly. 'Colonel Hauke was...he was by chance in the vicinity and volunteered to have a word with him before showing him out.'

Rachel grimaced irritation. 'It's too bad of Father Maguire to come sermonising at this time of the evening when we are likely to have guests. Has Marcus been bad again?' At Isabel's immediate, defensive look Rachel added cheerily, 'Come back to the drawing room and join us in a game of cards. Everyone was just starting to miss you...both of you.' An arch look winged Rachel's vision skyward.

Inwardly, Isabel cringed. If only her sister knew what had really gone on between her and her husband's good friend, there would be uproar, not raised eyebrows!

'I think Claudine and Vincent Ormonde would like the carpet up in the music room. They keep telling anyone who will listen that there are enough of us to make a set for the Barley Mow. Claudine has offered to play piano if Vincent will turn the music for her.' Spying the Colonel approaching them, Rachel interrupted her social plans to sibilantly whisper, 'Do you think he has been regaled with all of Marcus's mischief? It's very good of him to despatch Father Maguire for you.'

'Yes, isn't it...'

Earthy eyes grazed past Isabel's, relentlessly grim, making her sure Etienne had detected the sarcasm honeying her few words.

'We were just saying you must come back to the drawing room and make up numbers for a country dance. Your mama has said she will provide the music. But not for an Irish jig, I promise you,' Rachel reassured on a laughing breath.

'You'll have to excuse me.' It was a courteous refusal accompanied by a flash of a smile. 'I was just on my way to the stables, to check on my horse, when the priest arrived and delayed me. Storm threw a shoe in Waterford earlier today. I want him fit for the morning. Mrs Forrester has graciously agreed to ride with me on my last day in Ireland.' He slanted a significant look at Isabel, challenging her to refuse to keep the appointment.

But she wouldn't; she couldn't. Too much had been left unsaid. More than anything she wanted to finish what she had started and secure Marcus's future. 'I certainly hope your horse is uninjured, Colonel Hauke,' she duly sympathised. 'If it will help at all, I can prepare a poultice to ease the inflammation. Rachel's mare, Willow, benefited when her fetlock was bruised.'

'Isabel is a wonder with her potions, you know,' Rachel enthused. 'She was always stirring and brewing things in a cupboard at home. Our mother would wonder where she'd got to.'

'Rachel! You make me sound like a witch,' Isabel muttered on an embarrassed twitch of a smile. 'Next you'll have me casting spells...' She fell quiet, fearing she might have dug a hole to fall into. But it was too late. Inwardly she flinched at the malicious gleam in Etienne's dark eyes.

'Ah, now that I can believe,' Etienne purred with just a hint of viciousness. 'I think it very likely your sister is an enchantress, tempting unsuspecting souls at dead of night. She has the look of a siren, don't you think?'

Rachel clucked and flapped an elegant hand at him. 'Stop it! Look, you've made poor Bella blush!' Her eyes skipped between her sister and her husband's friend.

She thinks he is joking, that he is being delightful and flirting with me. The realisation made Isabel swallow a hysterical laugh. If only Rachel knew of the resentment behind his pretty words! 'Do let me know if you need a dressing for your horse. I'd hate you to cry off and leave me in the lurch. I'm so looking forward to our ride.'

Rachel's eyes became watchful as she sensed the atmosphere. She diplomatically wandered away to speak to Gallagher.

'Don't be so eager, my dear,' Etienne sneered softly as soon as Rachel was out of earshot. 'A woman who is no challenge can be rather irksome for a man like me. But then you already know that, don't you?'

Isabel felt the blood flare beneath her complexion. 'Yes, I do know that. But, unfortunately for me, a man like you is all I have at present.'

'That's excessive unfortunate for me too, Mrs Forrester,' he drawled. 'I never knew the fellow, but I certainly regret your husband's passing. Did he know the boy was a by-blow? Perhaps you were able to pass the brat off as his. Is that it?'

Isabel felt ice cluster beneath her cheeks. The lump in her throat grew until she thought it might choke her. How dare he term her darling son so! 'No, I didn't manage anything quite so clever,' she eventually whispered. She walked past him at once and found Rachel, linked arms with her, and suggested it was time to return to the others.

Frost sprinkled like sugar was dissolving beneath weak February sun. Patches of verdant ground were emerging dewy and glistening. Isabel stood on the steps of Wolverton Manor and surveyed the still, quiet vista as air crisp and invigorating as champagne bubbled against her throat. She took a deep draught, smoothed her brown riding skirt and settled her hat at a jaunty angle atop her thick fawn hair. The brave gestures did little to bolster her confidence. A small riding crop tapped nervously against a leather-gloved palm. Well, she could either meet him or return to her chamber. Heaven knew she wanted to retreat into the comfort of her cowardice. But she would not.

Her valiant little son was conquering his demons. And so must she. She had left Marcus being dressed by Noreen. He had looked solemn, but had got out of bed as soon as he was bid this morning. The wobble at his lower lip had wrenched at her heart as she kissed his soft shiny hair, then left him in Noreen's care to be despatched in good time for school. Father Maguire was her son's nemesis. Now she must keep an appointment with hers!

Last night she had received a note from Etienne, delivered by a gimlet-eyed Noreen. It had been just a brief instruction to meet him at eight o'clock. She knew he'd chosen such an early hour to avoid them being awkwardly joined by anyone else out on their morning constitutionals. She knew what his first words would be when they were far enough from the house to be private: 'How much?' He would want to buy back his ignorance of her and their son's existence. Of course, her price was far more than he would countenance paying. She was ready for his scorn on that score. With firm resolve and tilted chin she set off towards the stables.

Isabel was aware that Sam Smith and his subordinates were curious as to why she was taking a ride with a man who seemed withdrawn and careless of her presence. Apart from a terse 'good morning', Etienne had virtually ignored her while he paced and waited for Storm to be saddled. She had chosen to ride Fleur, half-sister to Rachel's mare, Willow. Fleur was a pretty bay with a flash of white on her nose and white socks. Despite her lack of hands she was a wiry little mare. Last time Isabel had ridden her she had been surprised that beneath a seemingly gentle temperament was quite a spirited, unpredictable creature.

Sam cupped his hands for her small boot, then hoisted her into the side-saddle. Once settled, she gave him a smile and thanks, then abruptly tapped the mare's flanks and set off towards the meadow.

As dainty Fleur leaped past the mighty black stallion it set the high-strung beast into a prance. She was vaguely conscious of Etienne cursing, taking the animal in a tight circle to calm and control it. After that was simple exhilaration and the wind combing icy fingers over her scalp, edging off her hat to droop on its ribbons down her back. Green grass, ice-spangled earth, brown denuded wood was a kaleidoscope of colour in her watery vision as she flashed past. It was so good to ride! If only she could fly on forever, beg the horizon to give her sanctuary, show her the rainbow she had long been chasing. She thundered on, heady excitement and apprehensiveness mingling, drumming an ache into her chest.

Fleur took the first fence that led to the brook in an easy soaring stride, then horse and rider came back to earth and were pounding away towards a sinuous snake of grey water fringed by skeletal poplars.

She knew he was close from the rumbling rhythm behind. She didn't turn. Her intrepid little horse was already slacking and Isabel felt guilty that she had urged the mare to such an early pace. Fleur was snorting gamely as she strove to outstrip the shadowy hunter, as though she also resented the preying males dogging them. With a rewarding pat to the little horse's neck Isabel urged her away to the left, let the supple stallion streak by, its hooves spitting turf back at them. She would have liked to veer off further towards the park and get completely away from him. But she didn't; she followed at a respectable pace and distance, as he knew she would.

By the time she caught sight of him again, by the stream bordered by sentinel poplars, the stallion was tethered and docile and so, it seemed, was its rider.

Etienne was seated on the gigantic bole of a fallen cedar that was precariously atilt, yet still anchored by fingerlike roots sunk determinedly into frosty soil. Isabel had seen the woody ruin before when riding. Again she felt sorrow that a magnificent specimen that had witnessed generations of hunters come and go was reduced to a fissured stump swaddled in ivy.

He seemed devoid of pity, relaxed and eyeing her over slanted silver at his mouth. He put the hip flask down by his side. A smouldering cigar was retrieved, replacing the bottle at his lips. She noted a pile of ash dusting dewy grass. He had been waiting some while for her. Well, she was here now, but he made no effort to rise and help her dismount. Isabel slipped easily from the mare's back and loosely tethered Fleur to a low branch.

Gentlemen, on the whole, politely refrained from smoking or drinking in a lady's presence. He was deliberately choosing to indulge in both. The inference was quite clear. He might not regard her as a lady, but then she certainly thought him no gentleman!

'May I?' An indolent gloved finger flicked at the metal bottle by his side. On impulse, begging a nip of brandy seemed suitably licentious behaviour for a hussy.

He looked at it, then at her. He held it out.

Slowly she approached, took it and had a minor struggle jerking loose the stopper. She had no need to look his way to know he was amused. She entertained him further by spluttering as the alcohol hit her novice throat.

Isabel gave her head a wakening shake. She faced him again, composed, and neatly replaced the cork. 'Ah, that's better. Thank you.'

'You're welcome.' He drew again on the cheroot, watching her through curling blue smoke as she placed the flask down close to his hip on the cedar stump.

She distanced herself immediately, but the image of him was imprinted on her mind. He looked quite handsome, she supposed, sitting there with the sun weaving colours into his dark brown hair. It was as well she no longer found him in the least attractive. It was as well a man with such a fine physique was an arrogant heartless deceiver, deserving only of her contempt.

Time today was precious. She was sure he must be as keen as she was to get this meeting over. The rancour that had raged between them yesterday again animated her mind, firing her pale skin with a pink bloom. Quickly she opened negotiations with a polite preliminary, and a nervous gulp. 'This isn't going to be easy for either of us, Colonel Hauke…'

'You have a nice way with understatement, Mrs Forrester,' he mentioned.

She cleared her throat, tucked some wispy spirals up inside her hat and settled it primly back on hair glowing honey-gold beneath the cold sun. 'I would like to start by saying…by suggesting…that we endeavour to be as civil as possible. Further malice and insults will benefit nobody, least of all Marcus. We naturally feel a mutual antipathy. I believe it should be controlled the short while we endure each other's company.'

'I'm sure you're right. I stand suitably chastened for my rudeness.' The words were correct, yet at odds with his impenitent tone and the gleam in his eyes. He gained his feet to begin walking towards her with some purpose.

'First I must say thank you for dealing so efficiently with Father Maguire yesterday,' Isabel rattled off, feeling compelled to pace away from him in the opposite direction. 'Whatever you said to him seemed to do the trick. He left looking quite content.' She took a glance at his face. There was nothing in his impassive expression to satisfy her curiosity. She waited. He remained uncommunicative. Slightly impatiently she demanded, 'Well, what did you say? What did he tell you about Marcus?'

'He said the boy is undisciplined, wilful and lazy. He also said that you won't allow him to be caned for it.'

'He's not! He's not any of those things! He's easily bored. And I...I don't want the spirit beaten out of him!' She spun on a heel to conceal her spontaneous angry tears. 'He...he is not a stupid child by any means. And I have not neglected his education. But he needs friends as well as lessons. Sums and verbs cannot be everything to a seven-year-old who loves to run and ride and explore. He is an intelligent boy...and he shan't be beaten,' she vehemently concluded her defence of her son.

'Did your husband beat him?'

Isabel caught her breath, hesitating momentarily before quickly shaking her head. 'Father Maguire seemed pleased when he left. What did you say to him?'

'I told him what he wanted to hear: that the boy will no longer be attending his school. I told him steps were being taken to have him educated in England. It's no less than a truth that will be implemented shortly.'

A silence strained between them. Eventually Isabel blurted, 'I have a right to be consulted over my…our son's future.'

The words were hoarse with shock, yet held such grit that Etienne smiled. 'Indeed, you do, my dear, which is surely why we are loitering about here this freezing cold morning instead of enjoying an early breakfast at Wolverton Manor.' He made a conciliatory gesture. 'Come, you cannot have it both ways: you cannot accuse me of deserting the wretch then fuss over what help I offer. He is behind with his studies and running wild. He needs reining in before it is too late.'

She was frightened; things were changing too quickly, racing out of her control. Matters that needed careful thought, things that she would have mulled over in her mind for days, were indolently settled by him then swept aside. But there was truth in his assessment of her son if not a shred of affection or loyalty. Of course her attitude to things would be different: she loved Marcus. She was sure his father didn't even like him. No, that was wrong;

he felt irritation, not dislike. No such strong emotion moved him where Marcus was concerned. For the most part he was indifferent to their son's existence. Could she hold him blameworthy? He didn't know Marcus, or her. They were all, farcically, intimate strangers. To gain a little thinking time she prevaricated, 'I thought you might deny he was your child despite the likeness to your portrait.'

'I'll admit it crossed my mind yesterday that a painting of a blond child that happens to be me yet looks like your son isn't conclusive proof that I've sired him. Neither is managing to recall the...*sordid encounter*...I think you like to term it. But I was intrigued by what the priest had to say about his mischief. If his looks and his character resemble mine, the two taken together seem pretty convincing proof that he is my flesh and blood.'

'Very magnanimous of you, sir.'

'It wouldn't be the first time a woman tried to pass off her dead husband's child as mine,' he snapped in response to her sarcasm. 'Another wastrel who had left his widow so poor she needed to go soliciting,' he muttered more for himself.

'You think my husband died penniless?'

'Didn't he?'

'It's none of your concern.'

'I'd say it is every bit my concern. I'd say your intention is to make your beggary a matter for my conscience.'

She strode swiftly close and a small palm cracked flat against a lean, tanned cheek with such a retort it seemed to echo away down the river valley.

'Well, that's a relief,' he drawled, briefly touching the livid brand on his jaw. 'I take it your righteous indignation means I'm mistaken. You don't want my money after all. What is it you do want? Are you out for revenge because you made no lasting impression on me eight years ago? If it still rankles, I apologise. If it helps at all, I'll admit I now can't get you out of my mind.'

'We were talking of Marcus, not us,' Isabel snapped in a low voice. She turned away from him to hide her humiliation. Yes, he'd easily forgotten her eight years ago. Now he wished he could. She knew from the irony in his tone that she and Marcus were a burr in his side, a distraction in his mind. 'There is more to this than simply Marcus's education.'

Etienne raised a lazy, quizzical eyebrow.

'There is much more to be learned in life than where Africa is to be found on the globe or why the Crusades came about or...or...'

'Or...that a basic knowledge of English and mathematics and other disciplines will be necessary for him make his way in life? The boy will one day be a man and must earn himself a living.'

'Yes, he will be a man, please God also a husband and a father. It's important he successfully undertakes those roles as well as being a breadwinner. He is a child who needs love to thrive.' She took a deep breath, simultaneously thankful and scared that their conversation had wended a path to a natural place for her to voice her demands. All she needed was the courage to brave his scorn and accept no less than was her due...for Marcus. 'He needs to feel he is part of a family...a proper family. He wants more than anything to be like his friends and have a mama and a papa. It is what he yearns for.'

Etienne's dark eyes narrowed on her pale, tense face. 'Before you say anything that might embarrass us both, let me remind you of a fact my mother inelegantly disclosed. I have a prospective fiancée. As soon as Miss Greenwood's father makes formal the financial inducement for me to take her off his hands, my betrothal will be announced. I shall be married shortly after and in due course shall be setting up my nursery...for my legitimate heirs. In theory it is all arranged.'

'Then I am sorry to be the one to foil your meticulous planning,' Isabel said icily, the tenor of disgust at his calculating quite audible in her tone.

'You shall not, Mrs Forrester, be very assured of that,' Etienne returned with steely confidence. 'I'll provide for the boy...and you too...but in my own way and on my terms.'

'Then we have resolved nothing here this morning, Colonel Hauke. I fear your terms and your way will not reconcile with my terms and my way.'

He smiled in a way that chilled her heart. 'Be more specific about your terms, Mrs Forrester.'

She immediately complied. 'I want you… no, I expect you to marry me and to be a good father to our son.'

'Restrict your ambition to those first three words, my dear, and I'll see what I can do to oblige you.'

Chapter Seven

'You think you've shocked me, don't you?
You haven't. You're probably also hoping to
have humbled me. Again, I have to disappoint
you, sir.' Ivory bone threatened to thrust
through the translucent skin of her knuckles as
her fingers clenched. 'I knew from the outset
that a man as callous and selfish as you would
expect something in return for any aid he offered. Aid, I might add, that he should feel
obliged to tender quite unconditionally. But
then I imagine acting morally ill behoves your
cold-blooded schemes.' She managed a tight
smile. 'What I am trying to impress on you,
Colonel Hauke, is that you must be quite mad
to think I would want you in that way or that
I would ever consider a permanent liaison with
such as you.'

'I have the gist of what you're trying to impress on me, Mrs Forrester.' A curt interruption and an offhand gesture supplicated for silence. 'My apologies in advance, for I risk being accused of indelicate talk to a lady. Nevertheless, to prevent further confusion, I think I ought to make something clear. In addition to an eager fiancée awaiting my arrival in London, I have also a dear friend. When I am married I shall continue to be very close to her. In short, there is no permanent role to be had in my informal life either. The only vacancy you might suit is in Suffolk. As you've already shown an aptitude for pleasing me, I would be prepared to oblige you with a residence there and a visit or two when I am in that part of the country. As to your son, I would be prepared to oblige him with a proper education followed by assistance in obtaining employment once he comes of age. I have contacts in the city and the army. Be assured that my supporting the boy is not dependent upon your agreement to become my sometime paramour. A refusal will not offend. All things considered, I think I am being more than fair and generous to you both.'

The effort of repressing her temper during his measured scorn had lividly blanched Isabel's complexion. 'I think you are the most repulsive man I have ever had the misfortune to meet,' she hissed. 'Why I ever let you touch me is a mystery, and will remain so, I expect, until the day I expire. Elm Wood must that awful night have been steeped in a noxious mist of henbane and liberty caps that rendered me witless. I recall feeling odd…hot…not myself. An evil force must have got into me…'

He gave her a smile that transformed into a long low chuckle of real amusement. 'Mushrooms and henbane made you do it! God's teeth! I've heard it all now! And before you fantasise further, my dear, it wasn't a fairy king that penetrated you that night; it was me. I did it. As for feeling odd and hot and out of control, that's not alchemy, it's lust. Trust me. I have some knowledge of these things.'

It was more than Isabel could endure. Her fears…regrets…even the shame that had tortured her conscience for eight years were being held up to ridicule. He must have a good idea of what torment she'd endured when she discovered at seventeen that she was pregnant and alone, yet it didn't move him one iota. Yesterday she'd been a damnable nuisance, now she was risible entertainment. Within raged a huge fire she knew was out of control even before the small feral cry rasped her throat. She launched herself against him, thrashing at his face, his chest, any part of him she could reach. If she was aware of his angry reasoning giving way to fluent cursing as he backed away, she gave no sign of hearing any of it. Her fists continued to flail and when they were finally restrained in a powerful grip, she kicked out with her booted feet instead. Deaf and blind to his savage appeal she fought on, white hot rage blasting blood into her ears and blurring her vision with wrathful tears.

Suddenly she was off the ground and whipped around, her spine rammed hard against his torso, her feet running on air. 'Put me down, you bastard!' she seethed. 'Let me loose or I swear I'll kill you. How dare you! How dare you speak to me like that! As though I'm some Convent Garden drab!' In her incandescent ire she hadn't noticed that he was carrying her towards a spinney. He dropped her close to a wide-girthed oak, positioning himself at her back so she couldn't turn without forcing him away. She attempted it, but reversing just inches brought her up against a masculine body as unyielding as the ancient timber chafing her breasts. As though to complete her imprisonment, two immovable arms barred either side of her.

Isabel rested her smooth forehead against rough bark. She allowed a small corner of her mind to register that she had behaved appallingly. Outrageously; in the manner perhaps of an unpaid Convent Garden drab. A residue of rage churned her stomach, but she felt too exhausted to stoke the embers and flare at him once more. She gave her head a small shake to clear scraggly strands of tear-damp hair from her mouth. 'Get away from me! I swear I'll scream if you don't leave this instant!'

'Scream, then. There's nobody to hear you. Besides, if anybody has a right to scream, it's me. I think you've broken my nose.'

Isabel's tensile quivering stilled. 'Truly?' she whispered. 'I have…I have hurt you badly?'

'Truly. That's quite a right hook you have. Where do you spar? I have a right to know so I can avoid the place.'

Even the wryness in his tone couldn't alleviate Isabel's self-disgust. Her shoulders slumped and her forehead again found wood. 'You shouldn't have spoken to me like that. I'm not what you think.'

'I'm not what you think, either. I'm not callous or selfish. I had plans in place for my future. In under one week you and the boy have turned my world upside down.' As though conscious he was explaining—justifying himself—he halted, cleared his throat. 'Nevertheless, I'm sorry I spoke to you like that.' A hoarse laugh stirred her hair. 'I came to Ireland to finally meet my friend's wife, not mine. Had I gone straight to London or Suffolk instead of diverting here to see them...'

'Eight years ago I had plans for my future, too, Colonel Hauke. Those plans didn't include living on charity courtesy of my eldest sister's feelings of guilt.' Isabel bit her lip. She hadn't expected him to dampen her ire so quickly with an apology. 'I don't mean to sound ungrateful; Connor and Rachel are very good and generous to us and take pains never to bring it to my attention. I know our situation could be so much worse.' She sniffed. 'Stumbling upon

Marcus and me must be the worst kind of bad luck for you. For me it is the most fortunate thing to happen in a very long while.' Isabel smeared her face clear of tears. Her jumbled curls were tidied behind her small ears and her returning composure put grit in her voice. 'I don't want anything from you. But I'll do everything in my power to ensure Marcus has a proper future. I made a mistake a long while ago when I was just seventeen. That's not his fault. I won't let him suffer any more. Not now. Not when there's finally a way to put things right. I hope you understand that.'

He made no response other than, 'If I let you loose, will you promise to behave?'

His sombre plea sounded hysterically familiar; it had been delivered in the manner in which she might address Marcus when he was fractious. In her fraught mind a despairing giggle racketed and rattled fit to loosen her teeth; in reality she simply nodded. The pressure of his body against hers eased. For a moment she felt too weary from exertion, too humiliated by her violent outburst, to turn and look upon the damage she'd wreaked on him. She slowly pivoted about.

He had backed off some way and was regarding her oddly. If she hadn't known him better, she might have thought his expression quite gentle. She decided pity had softened his features. He probably deemed her a quaint freak. Certainly the disdain that had consistently curled his lip today had gone. Of course it was possible sneering might pain him. She must have caught him quite a blow on the mouth for one side was already purple. A trickle of blood ran from his nose. She stared at him, as much fascinated as appalled as she surveyed her handiwork. 'You shouldn't have spoken to me like that.'

'I'm sorry...'

If only he had berated her, called her a spiteful ill-bred bitch. To hear him utter words which were her due, words which still stuck in her throat, was too much. 'You shouldn't have...' she croaked, then hung her head.

'Don't cry, Isabel. Come, the situation is not so grim. We must try to find a way out of this mess. Hush! If you are sensible, we can make the best of a bad situation.' His calm, patient reasoning had the effect of making her flinch so forcefully she folded at the middle. Instead of delivering a desperate platitude, he might have landed a blow. Again, she wished those kind words had been foul curses.

Etienne placed a light hand on her shoulder. It carefully, comfortingly caressed over fragile shoulder bones. When that touch was permitted he drew her into his arms, but tentatively, as though at any moment he expected her to revert to a fire-spitting termagant.

Instinct, honed from more than a decade of coddling temperamental females, made him drop his face close to her tumbled, tear-damp locks. A haunting scent drifted up. It was distinctive: a mixture of herbs underlined with a warm womanly note of a particular flower. A month ago the fragrance would have held a pleasant unidentifiable redolence. Now the blend was immediately suggestive of earthy, urgent pleasure coupled with the rhapsodic beat of wind and rain. The imagery was so complete that more than his memory stirred. A groan denied his reaction to being so close to her.

Isabel parted tear-spiky lashes to look at the bruised face angled over hers. The fierce heat in his sleepy eyes needed no explanation. It might have been a long time since a tinder-box and sporadic misty moonlight introduced that gleam, but she recognised it. Her eyes were again drawn to his swollen sensual mouth.

Etienne immediately focused on the same feature on her tear-smudged face. Her soft lips looked unbelievably full and rosy against the pallor of her skin. They parted, a small tongue touched and wetted the lower, and his eyes were magnetised by the nervous movement. His head was already inclining. Despite the acrimony that had just smouldered between them, it now seemed quite natural to want to explore what they found, this instant, mutually fascinating. And God knows he did want to kiss her…and more. The fire in his mind had blazed a path to his loins. He wanted her. He wanted a reason for the savage desire she could incite with a flash of those cool jewel eyes. But she wasn't so cold. Despite her frigid stance he knew she could be hot as hell and he felt capable of selling his soul to discover how quickly she would burn.

He's going to kiss me! The absurdity of it confounded Isabel for a moment. Part of her would have liked to feel his mouth again on hers, would have liked to know if it felt the same as it did in memories she'd nurtured until she knew by heart every breath that had passed between them. But the longing was crushed by the thought he might be simply testing that aptitude she once had for pleasing him. Perhaps he wanted to know whether she would be a worthwhile baggage to haul to Suffolk. 'Don't do it, it might hurt you,' she murmured with her eyes fixed on his ragged skin.

He smiled, carefully, with one side of that damaged full lip. It made him look roguish and vulnerable, far too boyishly appealing.

'I'll be careful…and gentle…'

'But I won't, Colonel,' she whispered, tilting her face to within a tempting hair's-breadth of his, so close that as she brushed past him she felt the soft skin of her cheek abraded by stubble on his chin. A light laugh mocked him as she spun about to look him up and down. 'I think you must be deranged to even try it. Perhaps I haven't made absolutely clear my dislike of you. Let me speak plainly. If ever you try to kiss me, I shall bite you. If ever you try to touch me in a familiar way, I shall hit you. Please don't make me again act in such an unladylike manner.' She straightened her skirts with an impatient twitch. 'But I'm very sorry I was…unnecessarily violent. I admit it was disgraceful behaviour. I should like to make amends and can mix you an arnica lotion for your bruising.' Her head slanted aside and she squinted professionally at his face. 'I don't think your nose is broken at all…just…' She trailed away into silence and approached him with a scrap of white she had extracted from the pocket of her riding skirt. She waved it up at him like a fluttering flag of truce. 'Here, take this to clean that there…' She indicated the place by touching her own face.

He took a larger cloth from his own pocket, rejecting her handkerchief with a bored, 'Put that away. Gore will ruin the lace.' He scrubbed unconcernedly with his plain linen at the caked blood, wincing momentarily before stuffing the dirtied handkerchief back in his pocket. 'It might not be broken, but it is throbbing like the devil.' The complaint was harsh and exasperated. That wasn't all that was pulsing fit to explode.

'Obviously you're referring to your nose.'

Etienne's eyes narrowed in masculine interest at her sly tone. 'Not necessarily,' he muttered, gravel-voiced.

'Well, it would hardly be your heart!' she sniped. 'I imagine even your so-close lady friend might have a task on her hands fracturing that. Either it's made of stone or you don't have one, just an abacus rattling beneath your ribs.'

Etienne stared at her, not knowing whether to burst out laughing or swear. 'We're at cross-purposes, Miss Purity. Let's leave alone the matter of what about my person ails me.'

Mistaking his raw frustration for an upsurge in anger, Isabel turned away. On trembling legs she hastened back to Fleur. She unhooked the mare's reins from a low branch and her eyes hunted about for a suitable mound for her to step upon to aid her remounting the horse. The ancient tree stump he had sat upon was too lofty and precarious to be used. As she paced back and forth searching, she informed him coolly, 'I'm afraid my terms remain the same, Colonel. You must accept that you now have the prospect of a violent harpy as a wife. I'm sure we might deal tolerably well together if we contrive to spend a minimum amount of time in each other's company. Needless to say, a nominal marriage is all I require. You may reassure your mistress that she has no rival in me. But I'm sorry that you must disappoint Miss Greenwood. Perhaps in time your treasure might understand that, in fact, it is no disappointment at all; rather a fortunate escape.'

A sardonic inclination of his dark head acknowledged the finale to her scathing. 'I'm sorry too, you seem to be under the misapprehension that I can be easily defeated either with female tears or a few lucky slaps. Nothing has changed, my dear. Other than if you try that again, I'll hit you back.' Without a word, and so swiftly it made her gasp, his hands girdled her slender waist and he hoisted her on to Fleur, leaving her to scramble for balance and reins. He strode immediately away and swung himself up on to Storm and without a backward glance spurred the animal into action and was off towards Wolverton Manor.

Two hours later Fleur clattered over the cobbles of the empty stable-yard, her hooves echoing metallically. After a moment looking about, Isabel spied the bent heads of Sam Smith and an apprentice over the door of the farthest stall. Both stared at her as she brought Fleur to a sedate halt close by. Sam was soon out and helping her dismount with a look creeping from beneath bushy brows. Isabel knew he was wondering why the master's sister-in-law and his good friend had ridden out together and returned separately. If he had noticed the marks on the Colonel's face, he would have little trouble guessing the answer to the conundrum. Etienne had ridden off in a foul mood; she imagined that in the short while it would have taken him to storm back to the house, nothing would have improved his state of mind.

Sam looked increasingly speculative as, with a pat to the mare's neck, he led Fleur away into the stables. The jet-black stallion was already blanketed and munching at his feed. As she approached, the magnificent beast ceased foraging and his head emerged over the top of brickwork. He seemed to regard her with a mellow, critical eye. She hesitated, then succumbed to an urge to feel the handsome animal's sleek thoroughbred lines beneath her skin. Warm sable slipped beneath her palm as she passed.

It occurred to her now that perhaps she wouldn't see Etienne again. He was due to leave Ireland today. Yesterday evening, when he had returned nonchalantly to the drawing room and the house party, he had taken his leave of both Rachel and his mother just in case there was no further opportunity to do so. His mother had been persuaded by Vincent to return to Ormonde Castle to keep he and his daughters company a while longer and Rachel had social appointments that were due to keep her abroad most of the day.

Isabel doubted he had yet gone. He would never allow such a prized animal as Storm to be sent on after him. He would wait until the beast was fed and watered and fit to travel.

Isabel stripped off her gloves as she made for the house. She could either give up her hopes of Marcus being reunited with his father or she could fight on…perhaps resort to blackmail. The thought horrified her, but then so did settling for Etienne Hauke's remote assistance. He would not renege on meeting the cost of supporting Marcus through to manhood. He baulked at being Marcus's father, yet would settle bills presented for his son's tuition with less interest than he gave to those received for his paramour's dresses. Isabel felt her temper stir. She would rather feed the birds with those crumbs he intended throwing their way.

She wondered if Miss Greenwood would want to marry him if she knew he had no intention of honouring his wedding vows. Perhaps she wouldn't care that he kept a cherished mistress so long as he was discreet. Perhaps she was no more in love with him than he was with her. Isabel knew marriages were brokered simply to merge money and stock. Personally she had always found the design behind it distasteful and depressing.

Etienne Hauke was a fortune hunter and seemed unabashed to admit it. The only valuable objects she had were her Aunt Florence's pearls and her paternal grandfather's gold signet ring. Her papa had sent the ring to York. It was to mark Marcus's first year of good health in a city recovering from an awful epidemic. But Isabel understood its true significance: it was to ease Edgar Meredith's conscience because, since Marcus's birth, he had wished his only grandchild had succumbed to the disease. If she had lost her son, her father could have buried the scandal in the same coffin.

Isabel entered the house. The thought of eating breakfast made her stomach curdle. She was barely halfway up the stairs when the Colonel's valet, Reeves, and one of the footmen appeared, carrying a trunk between them. So, the missing packing case had arrived. It was leaving almost as soon. The men grunted politely, if breathlessly, as they passed her on the wide curve of stairway. Isabel watched their slow careful descent with the box banging and swaying between them. She took another step before a glimpse of muscular legs and shiny boots arrested her.

He was leaving. He was calling her bluff. She could proclaim to the world he was a ruthless seducer and thereby draw loathsome attention to herself too, or she could act with caution and dignity and perhaps live to fight another day. Something akin to fear gripped at her heart. She banished it. He would not cow her. 'I hope you have a safe trip to England, Colonel Hauke.'

'I doubt that you do. I think you hope that the ferry will sink, and I will drown.'

'I would be a fool to want anything of the sort! Just yet, in any case, before matters are settled to my satisfaction.'

He positioned himself in front of her. An arm thwarted her attempt to sweep majestically past without deigning to comment further. With a simultaneous look over her head to ascertain if they were being witnessed he asked quietly, 'Have you calmed yourself enough to think sensibly about what I have offered?'

Isabel struck out with dagger-bright green eyes. But her answer was modulated to match his undertone. 'What you have offered is not acceptable. You have my terms. A great deal of sensible thought went into the preparation of them.'

A curse was expelled beneath his breath. 'You accuse me of being selfish, yet you would deny your son an education and good prospects because of your own wounded pride.'

'That's not true!' Isabel flared, with incautious volume. She whipped off her hat, the better to see him. Unruly curls were tossed back from her furious face. 'Marcus needs a home and affection as well as school and discipline. He needs a papa…and a family life. He is entitled to expect that from you! Please do not pretend you care about his welfare in any case. You would have quit Ireland without another word on the subject, would you not? In fact, you are no doubt greatly put out that I have turned up before you had an opportunity to creep away.' Her tongue-lashing was curtailed by a glimpse of an imposing figure she had noticed from the corner of a watchful eye.

Connor had wandered into the hallway, no doubt to investigate what was going on. She half turned to look properly at her handsome brother-in-law as he spoke to the men having a rest from heaving the burdensome chest. As Connor angled an enquiring look up the stairs, Isabel sent him a bright smile. 'I'm glad we have met, Colonel Hauke. I'm sure we shall again.' The hint of threat in her voice did nothing other than spark a lazy amusement in his eyes. One of his dark eyebrows curved quizzically. She understood the challenge: he might just as well have said, 'Do your worst; you'll never win.' With a bob she was soon past him and running up the winding staircase as though in the lightest of spirits. 'Have a safe trip...' flowed sweetly back at him. It wasn't until she turned the corner on to the landing that her fists raised and she spun about in despair as though looking for something on which to vent her furious frustration.

The Earl of Devane's carriage, as was to be expected of a rich and influential aristocrat's property, was jauntily sprung and its plump squabs were upholstered in supple hide. It was as sumptuous and comfortable as any fine travelling rig stored in the coach house at Redgrave Park. As the vehicle rocked over uneven ground the movement was rather soporific: Reeves was already dozing in the corner. Had his travelling companion been equally disposed to rest, he might have been sound asleep.

Etienne shifted irritably to the front of the seat, resting elbows on knees. He drew his feet in, examining the gloss on his boots as he tapped leather against wood in an irregular rhythm. The soles of his Hessians scraped impatiently away again over polished planking.

His dark head fell back against the cushions. From beneath a fringe of conker-coloured hair his aimless gaze flitted over Ireland's lush pastures. A low sigh whistled out between set teeth.

Reeves opened a lazy eye; it settled on his unquiet master. One side of his lips lifted. A hand delved into an inside pocket and brought out a travelling flask. He tapped the Colonel's arm to gain his attention.

Etienne curtly shook his head, annoyed as much by the intrusion on private thoughts as the damnable thoughts themselves that refused to be quelled or regimented. Immediately he changed his mind, relieving the valet of the liquor just as it was about to disappear back whence it came. Etienne winced as alcohol stung his cut lip. Over the tilted flask he noticed Reeves watching him, one beady eye fully open, the other nearly closed.

Etienne scowled, skimming the flask back so it landed in his lap. He had the distinct impression that Reeves knew what was vexing him. The fact that, early this morning, he had ridden out with a lady and returned alone looking the worse for wear would have spread like wildfire from the grooms to the other staff. It would be surmised that he had tried to take liberties with Mrs Forrester and she had defended her virtue a little too vigorously. Which was pretty much the truth, although her defence had come before his seduction was more than a glint in his eye. The intent had definitely been there. He shifted on the seat as his loins reminded him that, hours later, it still was.

He tried to sweep away time and a host of women and properly remember details that led to the most fruitful seduction of his life. What dominated his reminiscence was astonishment on discovering she had been a virgin. She had responded like a seasoned strumpet to whatever he suggested. He blocked any more thought of their feverish coupling and made himself concentrate on the outcome to it. They shared a history he had known nothing about. They shared a child. He had a son! His head dropped into his hands and long fingers grasped his scalp.

He was acting as stubbornly and stupidly as she was. Leaving without reaching an agreement was madness. He had had no intention of quitting the house without speaking to her again, of trying to reason with her again. Yet within a few minutes of them coming together the air between them had been thick with friction.

His meticulous plans for his future were disintegrating before his eyes. He felt resentful; in equal part he felt ashamed of his venality. Isabel Forrester was quite literally prepared to fight tooth and nail for her son's future. He was rueing the loss of wealth he would invest for heirs yet to be born to a woman he barely knew or liked. His eyes closed as he realised the gravity of the decisions Isabel Forrester was forcing on him. He barely knew or liked her either, but he admired her protectiveness, and God knows he desired her. She had shattered his orderly life in less time than it took to have a new suit of clothes made. And instinctively he knew that the pieces, once retrieved, would never fit back together the way they had once been. His life, whatever he decided, was irrevocably changed.

On impulse he sat forward, rapped out with his fist and bellowed for the driver to halt. Reeves watched him mildly, arms crossed over his chest as the carriage shuddered to a skidding stop. The shocked coachman probably thought the din heralded a disaster.

Etienne jumped down and strode to unhook Storm from the back of the coach. Reeves peered out, watching with a smile. He took a swig from the bottle. Well, who would have thought it? The disciplined Colonel, with his future carefully mapped out, looked like he'd lost his compass and didn't know which way to turn.

While they had been at Wolverton Manor Reeves had learned a little gossip about Mrs Forrester. He knew she was the widowed poor relation with a scamp of a son to contend with. For a man like the Colonel, with a shrewd eye to the prize in every deal, it wasn't good at all. But she was a fine-looking woman. Judging by the Colonel's bruises, she had a fiery nature beneath that demure exterior and wasn't settling for less than a ring on her finger. Any man would be tempted, even if it meant no cash and taking on a mischievous little wretch.

With a barked instruction at the coachman to turn about when he could find a suitable place, Etienne swung up in the saddle and gave a refreshed Storm his head. He travelled fast with a peaceful empty mind, and a driven primitive urge to locate the mother of his son.

He turned in at the avenue that climbed in a straight line to the house perched high above the coast. He reined Storm into a steady trot and wound a large rewarding hand into his mane, before caressing a warm graceful neck. It was as black silk skeins slipped through his fingers that he realised for days past he had barely given his mistress, Valerie Avery, a thought.

Chapter Eight

'When I said it would be good to see you again soon, I didn't think you'd take it quite so literally.' Connor rose from his chair with a grin on his face. 'What's the matter? Did you forget something vital?'

Connor's bantering tone failed to brighten Etienne's dour expression. 'In a manner of speaking,' he muttered.

Having ushered him in and poked the glowing coals of the fire with a toe of a boot, Connor settled once more into his desk chair, expecting to hear more. No explanation was forthcoming and his friend seemed intent on examining his dirty toecaps over a hand scrubbing across stubble. Powdery grime on his caped shoulders and silvering his dark hair suggested he had ridden back fast. The grim lines about his mouth were as much the result of weariness as the thoughts that were tormenting him. 'Drink?' Connor indicated the decanter. He grimaced, realising his letter to his attorney in London was now back with him.

A hand declined Connor's hospitality. Etienne wandered off to the window and stared out. His head and shoulders shifted, easing the strain in his muscles.

Connor's circumspect gentian gaze returned to him again and again as he removed the decanter's stopper. A sonorous chime was followed by a comforting lilt of flowing liquor. He sipped slowly, thoughtfully.

Connor already had an inkling of what might be distracting his friend and making it hard for him to leave Ireland. It was no fond farewell he had witnessed on the stairs earlier that day between his sister-in-law and this man. The attraction that existed between Isabel and Etienne had not gone unnoticed. He and Rachel had only last night discussed where it might lead. But lately a more disquieting atmosphere of conspiracy seemed to be drawing them together.

When Hauke had first arrived, Isabel had kept him at arm's length, although Connor had noticed that his friend made a subtle effort to slip under her guard. Now Isabel seemed equally keen for them to steal time alone. Rachel had been delighted that her sister seemed to be responding to their eligible male guest's interest in her. But Isabel was looking increasingly tense and contemplative. When he had disturbed the two of them earlier on the stairs he had again sensed something amiss.

Judging by the battle wounds his friend was sporting, their trysts were certainly full of passion but possibly not exclusively of a pleasurable kind. He was not sure how he'd kept a straight face when Hauke explained away the damage by saying he'd ridden into a low branch. The tale was decidedly implausible; the Colonel's horsemanship was renowned.

Contemplating a reason for their skirmishing put a crease between Connor's eyes. If Isabel had been approached in an unwelcome manner, then while she was living beneath his roof it was his duty—and not one he would shirk—to take his best friend to task over it. But Isabel had made no complaint and still seemed eager to slip away to meet him privately. She wasn't an untried maid, but a mother in her middle twenties. Connor's liberal views dictated it was not for him to interfere in her affairs until she hinted she wanted him to. Besides, he knew his friend; Etienne Hauke was judged by everyone to be a fair gentleman.

Oblivious to his friend's perceptive interpretation of his mood, Etienne paced the room. 'I want you to tell me about Isabel Forrester's husband. I know you hinted her past was not open to discussion, and I've respected that, but there are things I need to know. I don't even know the man's full name or what rank he held. All I know is he was a soldier. Which regiment? When did he die?'

It was an interrogation Connor had been half expecting. But the blunt manner in which it was executed took him aback. In a way he sympathised with this man's dilemma. If one were considering taking on a stepchild, it would be wise to at least know something of the sire's character and history. Unfortunately he couldn't help him at all. Nor would he if he could. Connor rose, went to the mantelpiece and carefully positioned his brandy balloon. 'I promised Rachel before we were married that what she told me in confidence about her sister's situation would never be repeated by me. I've no intention of ever betraying her trust, you must realise that.'

'I'm sorry to put you in an awkward position, it's just I need to know more about him than his name. Was he cruel to her or the boy? Why does nobody talk of him? Tell me, for God's sake! I have a right to know.' The words were blasted out in exasperation.

'Why do you? You tell me why you have a right to know anything about my sister-in-law. If I recall correctly, you intended dashing back to England not only to visit your mistress but to finalise a lucrative marriage contract.' After a tense moment Connor added gruffly, 'I can take a guess from what you told me that the business with Miss Greenwood is not indispensable. As for Valerie Avery, if your heart were in it, you would have made an honest woman of her years ago. It's no disgrace to overrule logic and let your heart lead, even if it takes you somewhere that seems unsuitable...somewhere you'd rather not be.' Connor cleared his throat and gave his friend a quirk of a smile, apologising for his unsolicited counsel.

Etienne stared at him as though startled by what he'd heard, then he strode to the desk and unceremoniously helped himself to a drink. The decanter clattered discordantly on a glass as he poured. 'You've missed your calling, Con. That sermon qualifies you for the pulpit alongside our friend Father Maguire.'

Connor grimaced at that; watched as his friend upended his tumbler and emptied it in a single gulp. 'I'm afraid I'm not done yet. I take it you are serious in this and your intentions are honourable. Have you and Isabel talked of marriage?'

Etienne propped an elbow against the window frame, five fingers scraped into his hair. 'Yes. We have spoken of marriage and God knows the situation is serious.'

'Have you asked her about her husband?'

'Yes.'

'And?'

'She told me to mind my own business.'

'You have your answer then. If Isabel wanted you to know about her past, she would tell you herself. Has she turned you down?'

'She turned down what I offered.' He knew from Connor's trenchant stare that he wouldn't be fobbed off with further ambiguity. He parried more questions by bluntly loosing some of his own. 'Did her father buy for her the first fortune hunter that happened by? Was Forrester willing to overlook the fact that his bride was pregnant with another man's child? I'd guess he simply took comfort in her dowry and ran through it as quick as possible. He's left her dependent on charity, hasn't he? And why is it you support Isabel and the boy? Did Edgar Meredith bankrupt himself burying the scandal?'

'That's enough!' Connor's voice was whip-lash savage. The warning hand he struck out formed a fist. One finger slowly unfurled, pointed threateningly. 'We've been friends for a long time now. I hope you're not about to act in a way that makes it impossible for that to continue.'

'So do I,' Etienne said softly. 'But I want some answers and if getting them upsets you…so be it.' He spun on a heel, and gestured a terse apology. He was acting boorishly; he knew it, but couldn't seem to stop. An inner rage seemed to churn his mind and body, obliterating rational thought. He knew Connor had every right to demand to know exactly why he was interrogating him over a matter that, ostensibly, was none of his concern. He was confused himself why the dratted dead husband should interest him to the point of obsession. One thing he did know was that he would soon lose his oldest friend's respect and friendship. He would wither a little beneath Connor's disgust when it finally emerged that he had been the scoundrel who had propelled Isabel into scandal years ago.

'What exactly have you offered Isabel? When you answer, bear in mind that Isabel Forrester is my wife's sister. Bear in mind that I am extremely fond of her and her son. While they live with Rachel and me, they have the full force of my protection.'

'How very noble of you. Or is it simply guilt? Had Isabel not accompanied Rachel to York when she jilted you and fled, she would have been safe from that marauding bastard who ruined her.'

Connor's stance was outwardly aggressive; inwardly he felt some relief. His friend was furious and exasperated because he'd discovered that the woman he wanted had been seduced and abandoned. God! He didn't know the half of it. And that, of course, was the problem: Hauke wanted him to supply the missing pieces. But that was for Isabel to do. 'I think you had better explain just how…just what you are talking about.'

'I think you had better explain to me why Isabel and the child aren't given shelter by her parents.' Etienne watched for a reaction. The slight flicker and flinch in Connor's expression gave him his answer. 'They've exiled her, haven't they? Why? They got her respectable.'

'Until I hear you say you've asked my sister-in-law to marry you, and she has accepted, you have no right to expect me to divulge one blasted thing about any of my in-laws.' Connor's voice scythed through the atmosphere like fresh-forged steel.

'One final, simple question. Where is she? I've searched your damned house from top to bottom for her. Gallagher thinks she's out, visiting friends in the village. Do you know where she is?'

Friction between them had built to a dangerous level, yet the fact that Etienne felt so comfortable having the run of his house mellowed Connor. It reminded him of the days they had once been more like brothers than army comrades or business associates. Whether carousing or campaigning, incidentals such as standing on ceremony for etiquette would always have gone unheeded by them both. He was about to say that he believed his sister-in-law had visited Clodagh Fitzgerald, when it became unnecessary. With exact punctiliousness a peevish child's tone could be heard in the hallway, followed by a woman's patient voice.

With an amount of incredulity Connor realised his friend was now looking oddly apprehensive. He was likely to drop his guard while vulnerable. Connor slyly pressed home his advantage. 'Why are you so sure Marcus wasn't born legitimate?'

'Because I was the marauding bastard who ruined her.'

The study door burst open and a child hurtled in, still garbed in his outdoor clothes. As though the exertion had overheated him, he started to pull at his heavy coat.

'Marcus! Come here, please. You may speak to your uncle later if you— Marcus, come here, at once!'

Isabel hastened into the room after her fleet-footed son. She was unaware her brother-in-law was not alone but in conference with another gentleman screened by the wide open door. 'I'm sorry, Connor. Marcus hoped you might take him for a ride on Sky. The grooms will not suffice this afternoon, it seems. I hope he has not disturbed you. Perhaps later…if you have a little time to spare…' Her flustered attitude kept her from immediately noticing that her son had ceased plucking open the buttons on his coat and chaotically weaving between furniture legs. Now he was standing perfectly still, his hat and scarf trailing the floor from loose fingers.

Isabel quickly turned to see what absorbed her son's interest. She froze statue-still just for an instant before carefully removing her bonnet from her tousled honey locks. Unconsciously she smoothed hair into place as she took a proper glance at her brother-in-law.

He too seemed dazed by his good friend's reappearance. Isabel wound the bonnet ribbons about a slender hand; the ensuing silence was only seconds long, but seemed to her to drag uncomfortably. 'Oh! You are still here, Colonel...' As soon as the phrase was blurted out she knew it sounded stupid. Obviously he wasn't *still* here; he had gone and returned. His travel-dusty dishevelled appearance was testament to that. She frowned, scoured her mind for something more intelligent to say.

'Are you going away?'

Etienne tore his gaze from the mother to the son. Lucid, wistful eyes climbed over him, pinned him down until the restless demons in him ceded and were still. 'What makes you think so?'

'I don't know.' Marcus shrugged his frail shoulders, his fair features contorted. With quiet confidence and a pursed mouth he nodded to himself. 'You'll go away.' His knowledge seemed to crush him momentarily. 'Sam let me sit on your horse.' Mischief sparked his tawny eyes alight again. Aimlessly, yet with a purpose that screwed up his sweet face, he whipped his scarf over the floor as though he would dust the parquet to death. 'He said I shouldn't tell you. Storm likes me. He didn't mind me sitting on him or stroking him. Do you mind?' The challenge was strong, hardening his glossy agate eyes and tilting his chin defiantly. The snaking scarf was tossed aside.

'Yes, I mind.'

Etienne saw the boy's bravado was fading. His sharp Adam's apple bobbed behind a tracery of blue veins on white skin. Long lashes fluttered as a consequence of his behaviour troubled him.

'It wasn't Sam did it. I…it was me. I got on Storm by my own. I jumped on his back all by my own. It wasn't Sam.'

'That's clever of you. He's very big.'

'I am clever.'

'I'm sure you are.'

'You don't mind I got on him?'

'Yes, I do.'

'Why?'

'You didn't ask permission.'

'But you would say no if I did.'

'Hush, Marcus. Colonel Hauke is…he is busy talking with Uncle Connor as you can see. Come…' Instinctively Isabel's fingers threaded soothingly through her son's platinum hair as she led him towards the door. He pulled away.

'Will you take me for a ride on Storm before you go away?'

'Yes.'

Marcus still stared up at the man, his expression expectant. Suddenly his face lit to radiance. 'I didn't really sit on him yet. I made it up...Sam said I mustn't.'

'Why did you make it up?'

'I don't know.'

'Do you often tell lies?'

'No...' His baby-large amber eyes swivelled to his mother.

'It was a joke, then?'

Marcus nodded and peeped beneath fanning lashes at his interrogator.

Etienne raised his eyebrows. His expression needed no explanation. Marcus grabbed at his mother's hand at the silent rebuke. Remembering his scarf, he stooped to collect it.

'Colonel Hauke! I thought you would by now be on the ferry.' Rachel, smiling widely as though pleased by the assembled company, entered her husband's study. A maid close behind was carrying her shopping packages. 'Have you decided to yet stay a while?' Rachel's voice betrayed her delight at the idea and her wide blue gaze slipped sideways to subtly encompass Isabel.

As though he had only recently surfaced from the stupefaction of knowing his friend had seduced his sister-in-law and had just been conversing with his own offspring, Connor rattled off at a speed that made his wife frown, 'Come, my dear, now let's away and find something to eat and you must show me what you've bought.' He took her arm firmly and turned her about. Over a shoulder flowed back at his nephew, 'Shall we find your pony?' With a fierce look at Hauke, he added, 'Marcus, ask your mama if you may come with us for tea.'

Marcus did as he was bid. A hesitant smile and permission were bestowed on him. Before quitting the room with his aunt and uncle, Marcus solemnly looked at Etienne. 'You won't take me for a ride on Storm. You told a joke as well, didn't you?'

'No, I told the truth,' his father told him.

The door had been closed but a moment when Isabel sent Etienne a reproving glance. 'If you're leaving soon and won't find the time, I'd rather you didn't promise him things he can't have.'

'I've not promised him a single thing he can't have.'

Isabel looked at him again, warily. She laid down her bonnet upon the desk and with brisk fingers unbuttoned her pelisse. 'So, why are you back, Colonel? Did you forget something?'

Etienne smiled at his hand, noticing it was still clutching an empty tumbler. The glass was deposited with a thump on the mantelpiece. 'Connor asked me the same thing.'

'It seems a natural assumption to make. Why else would you come back?'

'Why indeed?' he mocked himself savagely. 'Are you hoping I'll say I've come back for you?'

'No,' Isabel shortly replied. 'I'm hoping you might say you have come back to do your duty. I would like to think that somewhere within my son's father is a conscience and a vestige of morality.'

'It seems there is, Mrs Forrester, and my surprise at the discovery is no less than yours, I assure you.'

Their eyes locked for a moment and then he said with an amount of gritty irony, 'I trust you're not expecting me to go down on bended knee?'

Isabel flushed. He would never let her forget for one moment that he was coerced into this. Not now or, she imagined, in ten years' time, if they survived those years together. When she spoke, she hated the unshed tears husking the words. 'You need not fear, sir, that I will gloat or appear victorious. I've no cause for celebration. Neither of us has won. If Marcus gains from our union that will be enough...no, it will be everything.'

'Not for me, it won't. I have every intention of also benefiting from our union, my dear.'

Isabel swallowed, her complexion stained deep rose. 'I have promised I will not interfere with your life. You and your...good friend need not fret on that score. I only ask you to be discreet. So long as you give Marcus and me a fair amount of the respect and family outings that we deserve we should get along reasonably well. In fact, in time we might even become friends and that would be nice…'

His sardonic grunt abbreviated her sweet attempt at conciliation. A nervous raise of green eyes noticed he was genuinely, savagely amused. Isabel felt her humiliation burn as hot as the blood suffusing her complexion. 'It was just a suggestion. It isn't necessary,' she said graciously.

'Indeed, it isn't. We got the wretch into the world being lovers, not friends. In return for giving him status as my son, possibly my heir, the least you owe me is to keep the status quo.'

'I think it best we talk about it once wed.' Isabel picked up her bonnet and headed, with graceful aplomb, for the door.

'I think it best we talk about it now, before vows are taken.'

Isabel hesitated, swished about and glowered at him. 'Very well…if you must have your pound of flesh, Colonel, take it. But you'll find it not to your taste. Never again will I be that.'

Isabel thought he might scoff at that, but he didn't even smile. He simply looked at her for a long moment before murmuring, 'Once we were remarkably compatible physically. I haven't changed that much.'

'But I have, sir,' Isabel bit out sweetly. 'Copious wining and dining and the finest feather bed wouldn't now tempt me.'

A glitter of amusement narrowed his eyes. 'I might be a little older, more sophisticated in my approach, but I could still oblige you with an al fresco rough-and-tumble if you prefer.'

Isabel swallowed the wedge of humiliation in her throat. 'You are a most hateful man.'

'But still you want to marry me. Why?'

'For Marcus's sake.'

'Is that really all there is to it? What's best for the boy?'

Isabel turned away from the biting insinuation in his voice. He might as well have said: if you don't want me, perhaps my money tempts you. She opened the door, her knuckles whitening on the handle. 'Yes. That's all there is to it. Oh, one other thing. The boy, the child, the wretch, has a name and it is Marcus.'

Chapter Nine

'Did Marcus know his father?'

Isabel shook her head, chewing laboriously on a mouthful of succulent chicken as though it were coarse black bread.

'Did Forrester die when the boy was very young?'

With difficulty Isabel gulped down the meat, then neatly laid down her cutlery. A frown accompanied, 'There is…something I must tell you about that…'

'I wondered if you would tell me before we stood before the minister. It doesn't do to masquerade behind an alias at such an important time.'

'I hadn't thought of that,' she said meekly.

'I had, Miss Meredith.'

'Yes; I'm sure you had,' Miss Isabel Meredith sniped. 'Such a discrepancy might lead to an annulment. In which case I'm surprised you have brought it to my notice.' She overlooked the way a corner of his mouth tugged into an appealing smile. 'I'm sure you want to hear me admit it, so I will. I have never had a husband. The only man I have been close to in that way is my son's father. Did Connor tell you?'

'The only man?'

When she glared tight-lipped at him, he added, 'Indirectly your sister let me know. But don't blame her. I simply asked her your mother's maiden name. She managed to change the subject, but the look on her face was answer enough.'

'As you seem eager to have it confirmed, I'll oblige you with a proper response. My mother's maiden name is Forrester.' Isabel picked up her knife and fork again and sliced ferociously into tender meat. 'I shall refrain from asking how you appear *au fait* with ruses used by ruined women.'

He ignored the jibe, rolling the slender stem of a wine-glass between deft fingers. A liquid chocolate gaze bathed her proud defiance. 'I imagined you might find it difficult to sever every link with your mother and father.'

'You seem very perceptive this evening, sir. For that exact reason I chose to call myself Forrester. Despite my parents wanting me out of their lives, and Marcus, too, I found I could cling on to them...in my own way.' Her head turned, glossy curls jaunty about her face, shielding a pensive expression. 'I am not surprised you have worked it out. It is hardly original for an unwed mother to purchase a cheap gold ring, then seek a new locality and identity as a respectable widow. The subterfuge has doubtless been used since time immemorial.'

'You stayed in York a long time. Why? It must have held no good memories for you.'

'On the contrary: it held our Aunt Florence. Even as children we would plead to travel there and visit her. She was always our favourite relative. When Rachel jilted Connor and fled there she knew, right or wrong, her welcome was assured. Aunt Florence's home became my sanctuary too. Although she had little experience of anything outside the village she lived in, she was a great practical help to me and never judged me. If anyone hurt or maligned any of us, Aunt Florence would do battle with them.'

'I imagine she would have liked to kill me for what I did to you.'

Isabel's eyes darted from logs crumbling into the grate to meet his smouldering gaze. 'No. I never lied to anyone about what happened between us. You need not fret that I told my family I had been assaulted.'

'That was very brave of you.'

'Unnecessarily so; you never returned to defend either of our reputations.' She huskily mocked her gullibility. 'I actually thought some harm had befallen you to prevent you returning.'

'I'm sorry. Had I known of your condition…'

'It doesn't matter,' Isabel interrupted. 'As I have said, none of those first sordid details matter.'

'It wasn't sordid, Isabel.'

Her cutlery was dropped, impatiently, with a clatter. 'Of course it's not sordid to you now. Not now we're to be man and wife and you would like to restore a certain…*unity*… between us.'

His silence and heady unwavering gaze sent her attention dropping to her plate.

'What have you told Marcus about his father?'

'No lies, I hope. I told him his papa was a brave soldier who fought in the war against the French...and didn't come back.'

Etienne smiled. 'I think I can claim the honour. What was this paragon's name? He surely wasn't known just as Mr Forrester.'

'I took my papa's middle name, Luke, and my mama's maiden name, Forrester. My bogus husband was known as Luke Forrester.'

'My French grandfather's name was Luc. My name in full is Etienne Luc Thomas Hauke. I was named for both my maternal and paternal grandfathers.'

Isabel's lips twitched wryly. 'That's quite convenient.'

'Every truth will be significant, however small, when we endeavour to sort out this mess.'

'I know.' Isabel's voice was huskily sombre.

'I would have preferred Luc. Etienne was my mother's choice. I sometimes use Steven.'

'Yes,' Isabel cleared her throat and managed a wavering smile. 'Claudine admitted as much.' White teeth clamped on her lower lip as she noticed his narrowed eyes. 'I like the name Etienne…and Luc too.'

'And what are we going to tell the boy… Marcus?' he corrected himself. 'How shall we explain that his papa is risen from the dead and is known by a different name?'

Isabel's hands fluttered in hopelessness. 'I've no idea. I would like to tell him as much of the truth as is possible…without him despising me as he grows and learns.'

'Would you like me to broach the subject tomorrow when I take him for a ride?'

Isabel stared at a point on the ceiling, her brow furrowed in alternating consideration and consternation. 'No…I think I should speak to him first. But then…perhaps if we both together tell him… Oh, I don't know!'

'I'll speak to him first alone.' The edict was polite but quite firm. 'I would like to introduce myself to him without the risk of any discord between us erupting while I do so.'

'You think I will be purposely disruptive at such a vital time for my…our son?' she ejected angrily.

'No. It's not *your* behaviour I'm concerned for. I am not always the most agreeable person when at bay.'

'Indeed. I would vouch for that.' Their eyes grappled over the rims of two raised wine goblets that sparked candlelight. Isabel replaced hers. 'What will you tell him?'

'As much of the truth as I can without him despising me as he grows and learns.'

The servants arrived to clear the plates and the next course was served. Steaming platters of beef and horseradish sent a piquant savoury aroma to warm the lofty room. As the servants filed out and all that moved were giant fiery shadows, Isabel said quite gravely. 'I fear we have driven the Earl and Countess of Devane from their own home.' She sighed as she recalled that her sister and brother-in-law had suddenly this evening thought of an important dinner engagement that would keep them abroad. 'It must be difficult for them to comprehend such astonishing news. Rachel is quite overwhelmed. And I believe Connor isn't at all sure how he should react: whether he ought congratulate you or punch you on the nose.'

Etienne choked a laugh as two fingers went to test the solidity of the bridge of his nose. 'Luckily so far he has opted for the former. I'm not sure my vanity could take another battering.'

Isabel dipped her head. The memory of her tempestuousness still wounded her. In response to that she clipped out, 'If you had not behaved in such a…a vile manner…'

'Pax!' He grinned. 'I deserved it, I know. As I learn more about you and what you've endured alone, caring for my son, I know just how much I deserved it…and more. Do you believe me when I say that had I known you were carrying my child I would have come back?'

'I don't know. Now you're aware I'm of your social class, and related through my sister to your good friend, there is no other proper way for you to respond and still seem human. Had I been what you believed me to be, I wonder would you have worried that I or your child starved?'

'What is it you think I believed you to be?'

Answering that particular question was beyond her courage. Instead she demanded, 'Do you have other offspring? Perhaps you've no idea how many fair children that resemble your portrait are dotted about the countryside.'

'There are none.' The words were curt and he drained his glass as soon as they had been uttered.

'You said there was a woman who tried to pass off her dead husband's child as yours.'

He abruptly stood, shoving his chair back noisily against parquet. He strode to the fire, and hands that looked foreign gripped against ghostly white marble. In the darkling room his face looked devilishly bronzed by leaping flames in the hearth. 'I wish to God I'd never mentioned the incident.'

The controlled anger vibrating in his voice made Isabel flinch. 'I'm sorry. I've been un-forgivably rude. I have no right to question you over such aspects of your life.'

'Yes, you have, dammit! In a day or so you will be my wife. You have every right to know that and more about me. Question me about anything you like but know this: Marcus is my only child.'

He was quite sure that was the truth. Whilst in England he was faithful to his mistress. He had no reason not to be satisfied. Valerie Avery was an attentive and energetic lover who made it her business to keep him thoroughly entertained. In the army he had kept a pretty young camp follower in exorbitant style, which meant she had stayed clean and eager lest she lost her envied status to a rival. Not wanting the distraction or responsibility of a host of bastards, he had done his part to protect his women against pregnancy and let the sheets catch his seed. Which made it all the more curious as to why, eight years ago, he had abandoned sense and caution to such a disastrous degree with a sensual sylph who had ambushed him body and soul. Yet he had. He could recall quite clearly lying with her, their bodies entwined, in congress, as they recovered from a frenetic passion. He looked at her now, cool, solemn, poignantly sad because of that very coupling…

To chase the rising desire from his mind and body he demanded, 'Did my mother give you that miniature because she recognised I was Marcus's father?' His voice sounded rough and angry.

'No,' Isabel reassured quickly. 'It wasn't that at all. Claudine thought that I might have married your half-brother.'

'My half-brother?'

The outrage in his voice kept Isabel silent for a moment. She wondered whether to divulge any more of what Claudine had told her about her unhappy marriage. 'Your mother meant no harm. She simply recognised a family likeness between the portrait and Marcus. Naturally she would not think you were his father. She had seen us conversing quite normally together. We would both have needed to be consummate actors and thoroughly shameless to have done so, knowing our illegitimate son was asleep in the nursery of Wolverton Manor.'

'What did she tell you about Christopher?'

'That he was very like you; that you were of similar age and when young you could have been taken for twins. She said that when older, you grew darker and he stayed fair. I imagine that was why she imagined he might have fathered Marcus. The fact that he and his mother moved to York, where I was living, compounded her suspicions. Claudine knew I had lived there until recently and that my sham husband was a soldier. Your half-brother joined the army too, she said. These were odd coincidences so it was a logical assumption to make.'

Etienne stared into glowing logs. 'I imagine she has made my father sound like an adulterous brute while she was the wronged, dutiful spouse.'

Isabel was aware of bitterness in his profile. 'She admitted that they both sought comfort elsewhere.'

'How magnanimous of her to take some blame. It must be the first time ever. My mother always came first in his life. He would never divorce her so he lost the woman who loved him. He financially supported Christopher after his mistress married a wastrel. Christopher married and moved to the New World some years ago. I rather miss him, for we'd kept in touch until then.'

Not sure how to respond to that Isabel murmured, 'I'm sorry your parents were unhappy.'

'So am I,' he drawled on a breath of a laugh. 'For it could be hell on earth for us all.' After a very brief pause he added, 'He isn't able to defend himself so I will do it for him. My father was an honest, honourable man.'

'I'm sure he was.'

'Why are you sure? You didn't know him. Are you convinced of his goodness because he has such an honest, honourable son?' The self-disgust was apparent in his tone. 'Had my father been alive and discovered what I'd done to you, he would have been out for my blood sooner than your own papa.'

Carefully she said, 'I'm sure of his goodness because he has a fine grandson. I wish Marcus could have known him. He's never known the love of grandparents.'

'Well, he now has Claudine, for what that's worth.'

'It's worth a lot to Marcus. He knows so few relatives.'

'When he's older and more discerning, perhaps he might think that particular kinship not worth a jot.' He paused, gestured regret. 'My apologies. It's not the time or the place to trawl though family feuds. I know you've had enough rifts with your own family. I'm pleased that Connor and Rachel stayed loyal to you. Guilt or no over that damnable jilting that started it all, they could have abandoned you like the others.' He strolled to the window and stared out over sombre lawns. 'Have I your permission to take Marcus out for a ride tomorrow and introduce myself to him as his father?'

'Yes.'

He inclined his dark head in acknowledgement. 'If you'll excuse me, I have rather a lot to do if we are to be married before the end of the week.'

'Yes,' Isabel again said with cool dignity. *That damnable jilting* was the cause of all his ills. With sudden clarity she knew why he had been in York. 'Did you go to York eight years ago to look for Rachel? Did Connor ask you to bring her home?'

'Connor didn't know a thing about my pathetic meddling.' A soundless laugh rasped his throat. 'He was comatose through drink and fighting a fever when I left to bring Rachel back. The irony is they both escaped the consequences of my stupidity...you didn't. You were the innocent...in all of it, Isabel. And that's hard for *me* to bear. God knows how you've borne it.' He had gained the door and

Isabel was sure he was about to quit the room, but he hesitated and looked at her.

'I'm not going to lie and pretend sentiment I don't feel. But I will care for you and Marcus and I do want you…so much that it gives you quite an advantage. My desire to restore a certain *unity* between us, as you put it, would be a powerful tool of retribution should you use it against me.'

Isabel felt her heart pumping slowly at the raw throb of need in his voice. He desired her, but he didn't love her. Years ago desire in her had withered and died, stifled by guilt and relentless shame, but the yearning to be loved had flickered and endured. She stood, placing her hands flat on glossy wood. 'I'm sorry you feel that way. I think once you return to England and your…good friend…you will find the matter resolves itself.'

Horse and rider streamed against the azure skyline like a jet banner.

The panting steed was skilfully reined in until it trotted into the poplar trees then out again, winding a serpentine path through skeletal wood. Finally it clopped to a steamy-breathed halt. The horseman lifted the child from beneath his cloak to stand in front of him on the moulded sinews of the stallion's broad back.

'Turn around.'

The boy did as he was bid, balancing carefully, a wondrous smile animating his small face.

'Did he go fast enough for you?'

The boy simply nodded, for a delightful exhilaration had wedged words in his throat.

Etienne lifted his son, positioning spindly legs to straddle the horse so they sat face to face. With something akin to parental pride he scoured the boy's fair features. He was handsome, no doubt about it.

Marcus looked right back, quietly, without fidgeting.

Etienne let the reins drop and Storm ambled to the water's edge to forage.

'Do you recall that yesterday you asked me if I am going away?'

Marcus nodded, his eyes, his whole demeanour, gravely expectant.

'I am going away and so are you and your mama. You are both coming with me to England.'

'Does Mama mind?'

'No, she's glad.'

Marcus's solemn expression brightened. 'I'm glad too. My grandparents live in England. They don't like me.'

'Yes, they do like you,' his father told him huskily. 'It's me they don't like.'

'Why don't they like you?'

'Because I went away. I left you and your mama alone for a long time and that was wrong. I was away so long that people thought I had died and would never come back. But I wasn't dead, I was on the continent fighting in the war. Now I've come back.'

'Are you my papa?'

'Yes.'

'Were you brave? I told everyone you were brave.'

'Yes. I was a brave soldier.'

'The war was over a long time ago when Napoleon was defeated at Waterloo. Did you get lost?'

Inwardly Etienne smiled. For a child who paid no attention to his lessons, he knew a hell of a lot it would have been convenient that he didn't.

'Yes. It took me a long while to find my way home.'

'Did you fall out of a tree?'

Etienne barked a laugh. 'What?'

'Murphy's brother fell out of a tree and knocked his head. He forgot where he lived. His ma sent his da to find him. Then he got thrashed.'

'I didn't fall out of a tree, but I did get hit on the head.'

He lifted small white fingers and dipped his dark visage. He felt his son's steady touch press across the proud cicatrice beneath his hair.

'Frenchies did that?' Marcus asked, wide-eyed.

His father nodded. 'I did some equal damage to them. I was escaping and they tried to stop me, but I got away.'

'So you could come home to me and my mama?'

'Yes.'

Marcus looked fascinated and proud and ready to burst with happiness. 'My mama said my papa's name was Luke.'

There was barely a hesitation before his father explained, 'My full name is Etienne Luc Thomas Hauke. I didn't like the name Etienne for a long while so didn't much use that name. Now I quite like it.'

'*I* like it,' his son kindly endorsed. 'If your name is Hauke, why is my name not Hauke too?'

'It is. Your name is Marcus Forrester Hauke. Your mama called you just Marcus Forrester because…because Forrester reminded her of her parents and because she wasn't sure if I was still alive.'

'My grandparents aren't Forresters, they are Merediths.'

'Your grandmother was named Forrester before she married your grandfather.' This was no dunce he was dealing with. Etienne felt a surge of paternal pride. But before any further questions occurred to his sharp little son he quickly lifted him up and spun him about so his spine was back against his torso. 'It's time to get back. Your mama will be waiting.'

'Shall I say we went very fast?' Marcus's head tilted up over a shoulder as he sought his father's advice.

Etienne smiled and an instinctive hand cupped a soft rosy cheek. His immediate answer would have been: 'Let's keep it a secret.' Instead he said, 'If your mama asks then you must tell her the truth. But she might not ask…'

He kicked the horse into action and as the biting wind whipped against his face and the boy snuggled against him, warming his cold heart, he wondered how many years it would take before his son wanted to know why, when his father was escaping from the French, he had not yet been born.

Chapter Ten

'Am I vulgar and mercenary to have coerced a wealthy man to provide for Marcus and me?'

'No!'

'No? Even though he despises me for toppling his ambitions? I'm sure he thinks me a schemer with vengeance on my mind.'

'Who would blame you for that!' Rachel exploded. 'It is right a child's father should care for his own flesh and blood.'

'He would have more willingly done so outside wedlock.'

'He returned of his own volition to propose marriage. He's not past redemption. And he's obviously attracted to you still. Are you out for revenge? Had I been abandoned so long I expect I might have been out for blood!'

That morning's emotional parting from her sister was rudely dislodged from her drowsing mind as the coach swerved around a pothole. Isabel's eyes flew wide, focused, after rapid blinking, on the other two occupants of the vehicle. Neither was bothered by the bumpy ride.

Her son had coiled, cat-like, as close to his father as he could without actually reposing on his lap. Etienne seemed to neither welcome nor shun the small limbs imprisoning him. Even asleep her son managed to keep in contact with his father.

Before being taken off to bed in the evenings, Marcus searched for Etienne with a dogged determination that was heartrending to observe. No explanation that he was out riding or attending business in town would suffice. He needed to see him before he would settle. For his part, Etienne had so far been unfailingly patient with Marcus's foibles. She imagined he would display similar tolerance of an acquaintance's child.

At the start of their journey, Marcus had interrogated his father about his new home in Suffolk. Each lively question had been concisely answered. Just once on the journey Etienne had taken sufficient notice of Marcus when he continued to vault from seat to seat, despite his mother's instruction to sit still, to speak to him in more than a single sentence. 'Either you calm yourself or one or other of us must travel outside. As I'm not willing to incur your mama's wrath by forcing you to sit with Reeves up top, or hitch a ride with the gypsies, I shall need to get out and ride on horseback.'

Etienne had not once raised his voice; indeed, his tone disclosed his tedium at needing to issue an ultimatum at all. It produced the desired effect. Marcus had looked sulky, but settled back quietly into the creaky leather with his hands folded primly and his short legs sticking out at right angles to the seat. Within a mile or two his flaxen head was drooping against his father's caped chest.

Now Etienne was frowning out through the coach window as though a riddle of some complexity was concealed in the looming rain clouds leadening the horizon. Motionless fingers were curled close to his slanted mouth.

Isabel felt a surge of poignant frustration tighten her insides. Marcus was excited by the adventure, and overjoyed with his new papa. Etienne's lack of reciprocation hadn't yet dampened his delight. She and her son were travelling to a new life of comfort and respectability. She had got everything she wanted yet there was an emptiness where gladness and relief should have been. The man who had acquiesced to her demands looked as though he would extricate himself from the trap she had sprung as soon as he had fathomed a merciful way to do it.

She guessed he would, at this precise moment, much prefer to be flying ahead on Storm than to be wedged in a corner of a lumbering coach with Marcus's sleeping form draped over him. There was a latent energy…a restlessness about him that made his stillness seem unnatural.

As though aware of her observation, her husband turned his dark head and caught her gazing forlornly at him.

Isabel was glad of the fading light as she drew her cloak about her and turned her flushing face away.

'Are you in need of a stop before we reach the Red Lion?'

'No.' she said huskily. 'Thank you.' A nod indicated her drowsing son. 'Is he…do you want me to hold him?'

'He's no trouble…'

In response to his neutral acceptance of the burden that was her beloved son, Isabel managed a small faltering smile. It adequately concealed her inclination to quietly weep.

They were communicating at last and she would rather make small talk with him than sit in oppressive silence until they reached their night's lodgings. She settled on the first topic of conversation that entered her head. And indeed it had worried her when he had previously brushed the matter aside. 'You ought to have sent word of our marriage to your mother at Ormonde Castle.'

'Why? She'll find out from gossip soon enough.'

'As a courtesy, don't you think you should have been the one to tell her? After all, you promised she wouldn't hear of your betrothal second-hand.'

'Well, dutiful son that I am, I've kept my word on that score.'

The irony in his tone made Isabel chew her lip and regret her attempt at cordiality.

He raised a dusty boot, jamming it against the seat opposite as he eased his position on the seat. 'The news won't trouble her. At this precise moment she's likely to be more concerned with plotting a wedding of her own. I'd say she's successfully hooked him this time.' A sardonic smile acknowledged the puzzlement on his wife's face. 'Surely you realised she is Ormonde's mistress? She's long had an ambition to improve her status.'

'Why…why…no,' Isabel stuttered. 'I thought Vincent Ormonde was a relative of yours on your father's side.'

'He is. To give my mother her due, they weren't lovers while my father was alive. Ormonde was the richest man at the wake, and he'd left his ailing wife at home. He was persuaded to stay on as a house guest for a few weeks, to succour the grieving widow.'

'I'm sure Claudine needed a friend at such a time.'

'Indeed,' he drawled, his long lashes drooping as he sensed her championing his mother. 'She needed a very good friend. Someone generous enough to keep her in the Paris fashions she likes so much. My father's last will and testament settled everything on me with little more than a living allowance for her. She was rather irritated by that...until she spied Vincent Ormonde. Or perhaps it was the ruby on his finger she noticed first. I've seen smaller pigeon's eggs. Vincent has always been untroubled by good taste. Which no doubt accounts for his lengthy liaison with my dear mama.' He turned his head to gaze into darkness. 'It can be entertaining watching her homing in on some unsuspecting fool who looks likely to pay for the privilege of being seduced. I believe she managed that without too much trouble the night of the funeral.'

'Oh...I see,' Isabel ejected in a strangled mutter that brought his head around.

'Knowing you as I do, I find your prudishness quite unexpected.'

'You don't know me at all. And I'm sorry it offends you,' Isabel replied with quiet dignity.

'I've known you in the biblical sense, which is pertinent. Prudishness doesn't offend me; I could find it charming. Is it false modesty or are you really as innocent as you seem?'

'I haven't been innocent since I was seventeen, as you well know and are at pains to remind me.'

A flash of a smile mocked her prim indignation. 'Not all women lose their innocence when they lose their virginity.'

'I must bow to your superior knowledge on that,' she answered with sweet acerbity and turned completely from him, gathering her cloak about her and resting her head against the side of the coach. Her studied reluctance to converse further was ignored.

'There's something intriguing me even more than your naïveté, Isabel. Do you know what it is?'

'No,' she sighed. 'But I fear you might tell me even though I've no interest in your musings.'

'You're right to be worried about some of my thoughts,' he admitted through laughter in his tone. 'But I think you ought to oblige me with an answer on this. What puzzles me is what the hell you ever found attractive about an emaciated, shaven-headed young army officer who came close to trampling you with his horse and whose first words to you were thus less than complimentary.'

'I can't help you. I've yet to solve such an absurd riddle myself,' she murmured icily.

'I don't believe that. You know. Tell me what about me appealed so much that it made a beautiful, well-bred virgin allow herself to be such easy prey.'

The silence lengthened and Isabel kept her eyes trained on the shadowy woods. She shifted beneath his burning gaze. His bantering tone had been belied by a relentless demand that thickened the space between them.

'Come, tell me,' he cajoled throatily. 'How can I reproduce it if I don't know what it is?'

'You can't ever do that, so don't bother trying.' A whimsical mood momentarily transcended her embarrassment. 'It was of that time…that place…a fantasy…your white horse…'

'My what?' His mocking amusement was choked by astonishment.

'Nothing!' She was back to earth and turned to glare through the dusk at him. 'I don't want to speak of it,' she hissed with such vehemence that she saw Marcus start. An appealing look begged her husband to stop teasing her. 'Is it far to the Red Lion?' she whispered, as her son burrowed back to sleep.

'No. We'll be there soon,' he said softly, his eyes entrapping hers before they slowly closed and he settled his head back against the squabs.

Isabel watched him, studied his features of rough beauty, brutal still in repose. Breath wedged in her throat as she wondered what accommodation he had bespoken for them at the inn.

She had been married four days...and nights. Her husband had yet to properly kiss her, let alone consummate their union. After a brief marriage ceremony he had touched her on the cheek with cool, fleeting lips before his fiery eyes melded to hers. That look could have been stoked from desire or threat of retribution for forcing his hand. But he had so far left her alone and she was glad. Coercing a man to marry one was degrading; tolerating his loveless lust was much worse. Yet once she had, she reminded herself, barely wincing. But she had stupidly mistaken it for something else entirely—then she had thought she had found her soulmate.

The hero she knew by heart had incarnated from the wraith inhabiting her girlish imagination. Her love had come to claim her on his white charger, as she'd long dreamed he would. He was no stranger. Laughing together beneath his cloak as they sheltered from the storm, it seemed she had known him a lifetime. His charm and kindness promised an intimacy that appealed so much she felt, even now, the excitement twinge her insides. His touch had been as she expected...gentle yet strong; his voice one she recognised, cultured yet seductive. The first magical kiss was all it should be and presaged bliss and a lifetime of sharing. Why should she not have given him all of her? The magnitude of her pathetic romanticism still had the power to take her breath away.

Now she had shackled her gallant to her. A flickering glance took in his powerful strength as he feigned relaxation. Penned, perhaps, but he was not tamed...now or ever.

A quiet ceremony held in Wolverton Manor's small chapel had marked her victory. An Anglican clergyman had officiated. Connor and Rachel had attended but, apart from a small wedding breakfast shared by the four of them at the Manor, there was no celebration. And it was soon over. There was now a sense of embarrassment between them all. Connor and Rachel had wished them both well, and Isabel didn't doubt their sincerity, but because they were cooler with her husband than with her, she withdrew a little too. Oddly, when he had done nothing to demand it or deserve it, she yet behaved loyally to her spouse.

She had felt quite sure that her debonair bridegroom would claim his reward for giving her and her son his name and protection. But despite his frequent intense glances as the hour grew late, he had not, as she feared, attempted to beat a path through their dressing room into her bolted chamber on their wedding night. Perhaps he had not wanted to outrage their hosts with any uproar as he exerted his conjugal rights. Perhaps he simply had not wanted her as much as he had said.

The following few days spent at Wolverton Manor had been busy with preparation for departure. They easily avoided each other until they dined in the evening and four people blithely strove to maintain an adequate amount of conviviality during six courses.

After dinner the bride would visit the nursery to see her sleeping son before she retired.

From the lack of noise in her husband's adjoining chamber, Isabel knew he came late to bed. On one occasion it appeared he did not retire at all, but instead went into town carousing. On her way down to breakfast Etienne had been on his way up the stairs. He had looked quite outrageously dissolute with his long dark hair tangled and his concave cheeks appearing yet more hollow, shaded with stubble. His jacket, hooked on a finger, had hung neglected over a shoulder in a condition likely to give his valet a fit. They had barely exchanged a greeting as they passed, like the strangers they were. It was only as she sat watching her tea rock in her cup at the breakfast table that Isabel realised her sleepy-eyed bridegroom might have spent the night with a local woman.

They were man and wife, yet no bond of affection existed between them—just a simmering sexual awareness that coloured each word and glance. With a woman's instinct Isabel knew that the restraint he was imposing on himself was responsible for his detachment. If she punished him with coldness, he would retaliate in his own way.

Her eyes closed wearily. She was prepared for difficulties, she told herself, attempting to empty her chaotic mind and feel peaceful enough to catnap a while. It was no proper marriage, but she had got her son his father and his future, and that was all that mattered.

It was the icy draught that woke her. Isabel came to with a start, her drowsy mind still haunted by men with creased brown visages who steered a vehicle daubed with many colours. Nervous and barely conscious, she slid along the seat to grab at the carriage door, slightly ajar and whining on its hinges in a bitter breeze. She peered out of the window, blinking at the whitewashed building with low serpentine roofline and four fiery square panes promising a warm welcome.

Spying Reeves by the horses' heads, she called to him softly so as not to wake Marcus still asleep on the seat. Her husband was nowhere to be seen.

'Have we reached the Red Lion?'

'Yes, we have, Mrs Hauke.' The valet parted from the ostler, to whom he'd been chatting, and hurried towards her.

'Are the gypsies still close?' Isabel demanded. The residue of her nightmarish dream about the band of travellers they had passed on the road earlier that day still disturbed her. Three patterned wagons had followed them at a distance for some miles along the isolated track before they were lost to view.

At one point a caravan had got close enough for Isabel to see the leathery faces of the men who sat on the driver's seat. She'd also observed the fierce-featured woman who sat between them, gold hoop earrings protruding from beneath a red shawl that was also protecting her hair from the elements. Something about their intent black eyes had alarmed Isabel. But Marcus had been delighted by the spectacle and had poked his blond head out of the window to wave at them before she had time to restrain him. She had instinctively sought to shield him from view and suddenly she knew why: gypsies were rumoured to abduct young children.

Etienne had seemed unperturbed and faintly amused by their fascination as though, for him, the sight of such tribes on the highways and byways was fairly commonplace.

'You don't want to be getting worried about those sort of folk, Mrs Hauke,' Reeves reassured her. 'They scavenge about the farms and hedgerows but won't come bothering gentry unless they have bits and bobs to sell.' Briskly he rubbed together his gloved palms. 'A chilly night it is, to be sure. Ah, here comes the Colonel now.' The valet nodded at a tall shadowy figure striding from the inn towards the coach.

Etienne reached in and scooped Marcus into his arms. 'They have a clean chamber ready and decent food. I've ordered a meal to be served in the annexe and hot water to be prepared.' He stood aside for Isabel to alight. With Marcus cradled against his chest, he followed her into the inn.

'Where is Etienne?'

'I expect he is settling with the innkeeper for the food we have eaten. It was tasty, was it not? Are you full?'

Marcus nodded, simultaneously ducking his face away from the washing cloth. Isabel put a controlling hand on his flaxen head. 'Keep still, please! You have gravy on your chin.'

Finished with wiping his face, she turned her attention to his grubby hands. Steam rose from the warm water the landlady had provided. 'Rinse your hands,' she instructed her son and he did so, purposefully splashing some water into her lap and soaking her gown. With an exasperated little huff, Isabel caught at his wriggling fingers and towelled them. With an inner grimace she realised her son was probably too lively to settle down to sleep now he had enjoyed an hour or more of repose in the coach.

'Into bed with you!' She clapped her hands playfully to hurry him, then blew out the candle by the cot positioned to one side of a high four-poster bed.

Isabel eyed the bed apprehensively. It was layered in white linen with a good thick quilt spread on top. As her son slid beneath his pristine bed sheets, Isabel pulled back the covers on the four-poster, testing the firmness of the mattress. There was nothing to complain about at all. The food they had eaten had been ample and delicious, the chamber was spacious and spotless, the landlady, Mrs Broome, had been friendly and cooperative. Mr Broome had vowed, with a discoloured grin, that he had given the lady the best room to be had anywhere in the county.

It was also the only room he had to bestow. A party of raucous dandies enjoying a local shoot had taken the other chambers. One of the gentlemen had recognised Etienne and had struck up conversation with him just as Mrs Broome led her and Marcus away along the corridor to the quiet annexe she kept for Quality.

Isabel imagined her husband's lengthy stay below stairs in the taproom was not simply a courtesy to allow her time to suitably attire for the night. Possibly he was content to enjoy better company than he would find with her. She didn't want him to join her upstairs. Yet for no reason she could understand, being abandoned pricked her bride's vanity.

Isabel opened her travelling bag and pulled out an embroidered white night rail. He might like his foppish friends better than her, but she doubted he would stay with them the night through. He needed a good night's rest as much as she did. But it would need to be a wicked man who would expect more than sleep tonight when their child lay barely a yard away. Etienne was not that.

Slipping out of her dusty travelling clothes, she folded them neatly, then washed in the herbal washing water.

'Where is Etienne?'

'Hush, go to sleep, Marcus,' Isabel purred as she tied the ribbons of the cotton nightgown.

'Where *is* he?' Marcus demanded querulously, sitting upright in bed and looking at his mother through the guttering tallow.

'He is taking a drink with the hunters. And he must pay the innkeeper, too, for our dinners.'

'You said he has already paid that fat man. Will he go away and leave us? I don't like it here.'

Isabel sat on her son's narrow bed and soothed him with a cool lavender-scented hand. 'Lay down, dear. Your papa won't leave you, I promise. He is taking us to our new home. Can't you hear the gentlemen laughing in the bar? Listen! They are chatting and clinking their glasses of beer.'

'Don't blow out that candle,' her son entreated in a thin voice. His head dipped at the one solitary flame still burning.

'I won't, I promise. Now go to sleep,' she crooned.

Marcus descended into his sheets, a thumb at his pouting mouth.

Isabel watched him from a chair until his small ribs were rising and falling rhythmically. She turned the key in the lock then placed it on a hook by the door. Etienne had in his possession a similar key to the room. Obliquely she realised the noise in the bar had quietened. She gratefully sank into soft down and stared up at the brocade canopy overhead. It was damson coloured with heavy tassels and looked familiar. Just before exhaustion claimed her, she realised the canopy resembled the shawl the gypsy woman had used to cover her raven hair.

Isabel awoke with a start and instinctively turned towards where Marcus slept. Icy fear was squeezing her heart even before she properly focused on her son's empty bed.

Her sheets and blankets were tossed back and in an instant she was simultaneously searching for her slippers and thrusting her arms into her wrap. The key had gone from its hook and without thought for propriety she was, flimsily attired, risking observation on the landing. The flickering stump of candle grasped in her hand was in danger of extinguishing, so hastily did she dash back and forth along the creaky boards while repeatedly hissing a whispering call to her son.

'Gawd! Do leave off! He ain't in 'ere. This one's name's Jack be all accounts,' shrieked a coarse female voice. A vulgar giggle was joined by a rumbling male chuckle, then other sounds that made Isabel's cheeks flame and hastened her flight to the head of the stairs.

Isabel sped below, frightened to call Marcus again lest she attracted further unwanted attention to herself. She raced along a beam-blackened corridor and yanked at a door. The squat snug contained just the smell of stale ale and cheap tobacco. She quit the room quickly to continue her hunt. The next room was silent but for the shifting of a few embers in the grate. Eerie shadows leapt upon the walls and

a fitful flame illuminated a couple of abandoned tankards. The last room she dashed
within, she disturbed a trio of grizzled men
silently playing cards. In unison they turned to
stare grimly and aim their clay pipes at her.
She backed away, tears coagulating in her
throat, as irrational fear squeezed her heart.

Her son was gone, and so too, it seemed,
was her husband. Not properly awake, reason
was impaired and her imaginings became fe-
verishly hysterical. It would suit him to dis-
pose of the inconvenience that was their son,
and abandon her. He wanted rid of them both.
And gypsies were close by. Had he not said,
but for her presence, he would have put
Marcus out on the road to hitch a ride with
those heathens? Suddenly she felt petrified and
certain of her sweet son's fate. Her husband
had stolen Marcus while she slept and taken
him off to be sold to gypsies. And she was
alone, in England, with little money and no
friends. How would she find him? Or buy him
back? She yanked open the door at the end of
the corridor and a blast of icy air whipped her
thin night rail back against her legs. 'Marcus!'
she shrilled in desperation and stood shivering

as she surveyed a bleak landscape of moon and frost silvered soil. She had barely put a slippered foot outside when a gripping hand arrested her and spun her about.

'What the hell are you doing?'

Chapter Eleven

'What are *you* doing?'

Her uncontrollable quivering, part shock on being startled, part fury at his imagined wickedness, sent a riot of fawn ringlets dancing about her slender white shoulders. 'What have you done with my son?'

The door was rammed shut and a draught of icy air swirled about her ankles, billowing her nightclothes away from her unsteady legs. She was trapped against the wall by his aggressive stance, her narrow fleshless back, little protected by cambric, adhering to clammy distemper. 'And where have you been all this time?' she stormed, biting back tears.

From between close black lashes his eyes glittered at her, pinned her down. 'Where have I been? I've been keeping my undesirable person out of your bed, my dear, which is what I imagined you wanted.' Etienne's gaze was involuntarily drawn from her wan face to the allure of a pert bosom heaving a mere shiver from his chest. 'As for our unattended son, he found me some hours ago playing dice with an acquaintance in the annexe. I would have returned him to you, but I anticipated my arrival in your bedroom might have earned me a slap for my pains. Besides, Marcus was reluctant to go and said you were asleep. I decided to leave well enough alone as he soon settled down on a chair.'

Isabel felt relief and shame clog her throat. She should have known her son wouldn't properly settle until he located his father. His child's intelligence had led him back to where he had last been with Etienne—Mrs Broome's best parlour in the annexe. In a frenzy of prejudice she had convinced herself the taprooms would be where her grudging reprobate of a husband was to be found. A shuddering indrawn breath preceded, 'Good. I'm glad he is safe and sound.' She attempted to sweep past, a hand swiping wet from her lashes before it became obvious. Two palms slammed against the wall either side of her, imprisoning her.

'You asked me what I'd done with your son. What did you imagine I'd done? Abducted him? Murdered him?' Arrant scorn coloured his glare, then faded from his eyes to be replaced by fury. 'My God! You did! You believe I'd harm him.'

'No!' Isabel blurted, but found she couldn't compound the lie. Instead her fingers gripped at his sleeves, shook at the material in her desperation to make him understand. Never had she seen him look so savage. Even when she had lashed out at him, cornered him into a marriage he didn't want, he had not been so obviously enraged. 'I was so frightened when I found him gone. I remembered the gypsies. They take children. I couldn't find you either. I needed you, but you were nowhere to be seen.'

His eyes lowered insolently to the slender body trembling beneath *broderie anglaise.* As a nasty laugh scratched his throat, Isabel caught the sweet scent of alcohol breezing past.

'Well, I'm here now, Isabel, do you still need me?'

A barely perceptible shake of her head denied him. Her fingers, finished with spoiling the fine material of his sleeves, sprang over solid forearms in a vain attempt to move them.

'Well, it's a pity you do not,' he murmured hoarsely. 'Because, God knows I need you. You make my blood boil and not simply because you deem me capable of disposing of my own child. In truth you're the one I'm likely to throttle, my dear. If I resist that urge I might instead trade *you* to the Romanies, if I can persuade them to take such a shrew. But that's for later. We made a bargain. I've kept my side of the deal, now it's your turn.' He removed the candle from her grip and placed it on a table close by.

Isabel instinctively ducked to escape and retrieve it. She was entrapped and immediately put back against the wall. 'Be sweet to me,' he mocked, velvet-voiced. 'I have a very bitter taste in my mouth.'

'That's because you've drunk too much,' Isabel snapped, yanking at his wrists. The muscles beneath her fingers flexed, but he remained unmoved.

'I'm sober enough to consummate my marriage. It's time we had our honeymoon. Not the choicest venue for a romantic wedding night, but needs must when the devil drives. And I am the devil, sweet, aren't I?'

Isabel felt the fight go out of her. The small fingers, clamped on his brawny forearms, relaxed. He was incensed and with good reason. She had treated him awfully…again. 'No, you're not the devil,' she whispered. 'So far, you've treated us both well. Please don't spoil it. I awoke with a start after dreaming again of those travellers. I panicked when I couldn't find Marcus and imagined harm had befallen him.' She attempted a smile. 'I know it's stupid, but I've never before seen such grim-faced people and I cannot put them from my mind.'

Etienne's head lowered, an abrasive cheek grazed the soft skin of one of hers, nudging so her mouth closed with his. 'Forget them. You've cast *me* in the role of villain tonight and I'm ready to oblige you. Play the part of a sweet innocent. That would definitely oblige me…' His mouth slyly lunged, but she quickly averted her face, presenting him with a screen of softly coiled ringlets.

'Let me pass. Marcus needs me more than you do.'

'He's fast asleep.'

'He'll get cold and catch a chill.'

'He's covered with blankets.'

'He hates being alone in the dark.'

'He's got a brace of candles and my friend Thadeus Staines snoring in a chair to keep him company.'

Isabel ceded. She turned her head just a notch until the warm brandy breath on her cheek warned her to be still. She'd hurt him badly by thinking him capable of such dastardly behaviour. Far from harming Marcus, it seemed he had cared well for him. So far he had cared well for her too. Was that about to change? She rallied her courage; she was no more intimidated by him now than when she had confronted him over their son's future, she told herself. Whipping her head about, she glared up into eyes like embers. 'You know I have already told you what will transpire if you try to kiss or touch me.'

'You wouldn't fight me for long, Isabel, we both know that.' The smile he gave her was breathtakingly confident.

'I'm sorry you're inebriated enough to think that.' Barely a tremor betrayed the worth of the warning.

'And I'm sorry that I've acted the perfect gentleman since our marriage in the risible hope you might appreciate my noble restraint. You've always believed me a heartless degenerate. Now I've a mind to act like one.'

A dark hand moved up, a single firm finger outlined her sharp chin. The touch was teasingly light; she could have easily slapped it away. Yet she felt enchanted by the lulling sensation and her breath caught in her throat. Her lowered eyes followed that single digit out of sight. At the same moment it traversed to skim a breast she sought to escape. Dark hands clasped about her nape and two thumbs flicked her face up to his.

His mouth was hot and hard, his tongue silken, teasing at the clamped line of her lips. A solid thigh insinuated between her legs, tipping her craftily, almost imperceptibly, so her groin chafed on its rocky sinews. A tussle ended in her being overwhelmed while the onslaught on her mouth continued, veering between selfish demand and slick seductive skill.

Dew was dilating her lips and pelvis, draining her of resistance, chilling then heating blood that throbbed with urgent decadence about her pliant body. She felt herself lifted, her limbs guided, moulded to fit about his. A hand smoothed along the feverish satin of her inner thigh, drawing cambric in its wake. And then it was over. She was on the ground, back against the wall, her feeble palms cupping plaster to keep her upright.

Isabel blinked into darkness, her lungs heaving as she fought to calm her racing heart. She bit her lip to stop herself calling him to come back. His dark clothes made it difficult for her to locate his silhouette at all in the corridor, then what was left of her candle stump illuminated his lean profile at a distance.

'I'm hungry. Will it be soon time for breakfast?'

'Yes…not long. Your mama has been looking for you.'

The disembodied words haunted the hallway. Etienne turned, beckoned, and the candle stump's weak flame revealed the boy now in his arms.

She obeyed him automatically, gliding forward at the signal, a ghostly figure in the gloomy corridor.

Etienne drew her close, an arm about her shoulders. It tightened on her at once, perhaps to warm her, perhaps to prevent her pulling away. Despite the battle between them just moments before, rejecting him now had not occurred to her.

'There's yet time for us all to get some sleep before we journey on,' Etienne said quietly. 'Tomorrow will be a long day of travelling.'

'I'm hungry…'

'We have some biscuits in the chamber and an apple. That must suffice, Marcus, until it is light.' Isabel finally found her tongue. She cleared her throat, hoping the quaver in her voice was banished too. 'You should not have left the room. I'm very angry with you. Where is the key? Give it to me.'

Marcus pointed back towards the annexe, from whence he had come.

'I have a key,' Etienne interjected peaceably. 'Come, apologise to your mama for worrying her.'

Marcus did so, albeit with his bottom lip thrust petulantly. Isabel stole a quick look at her husband. Just his eyes were in light; she would have needed to shift the taper to gauge the rest of his expression. At the back of his steady regard was a hint of apology, but as their eyes entwined, he allowed desire bold precedence. The candle wavered and she saw the slow smile that was intensely self-deprecating. He took her elbow and steered her towards the stairs.

In what was left of the night, Isabel woke just once. She blinked herself to awareness when the covers resisted being pulled up to her chin to ward off the fierce fireless chill.

Etienne's fully clothed weight was firmly anchoring the quilt. Isabel wriggled down carefully into warmth, blinking at the dusky male head on the pillow next to hers. By the light of the candle she studied him from beneath heavy lids with a rapt fascination.

Now, at last, she could yearn for the boy she'd once known. In repose he looked much younger...sweeter. Elemental grooves that bracketed his mouth and radiated from the sun's attack seemed less noticeably etched in his skin. Five long fingers curled against his temple looked anything but brutal. His face was angled slightly away from her; long mahogany hair rippled back in skeins from his skull as though a hand had recently raked though it. Isabel squinted, but it was too luxuriant to betray pale skin in the half-light. A nervous finger tiptoed to slink within, slip feather-light over his scalp.

She shrank back with a gasp, but those innocent-looking digits had already imprisoned her wrist. With imperceptible speed he had rolled on to his front and was rearing on an elbow over her. Her impertinent hand was thrust down on the pillow above her head. 'It's a bit late to be seeking proof.' A significant glance incorporated the child slumbering in the cot next to the bed. The fingers straining in his for release were brought to his mouth, mockingly saluted. Just one was shoved across the jagged scar on his scalp, then flung from him immediately as though it were a burning brand.

'Satisfied?' He flopped on to his back with a grunt of stark sarcastic laughter.

Isabel hadn't the temerity to ask what amused him.

'Don't touch me, Isabel. Not in anger or curiosity. And never while lying beside me in bed unless…' The sibilance died away, incomplete, and in a move that was isolating, his hand rose again to his temple and his face averted. A leg drew along the quilt, bent at the knee. The barrier between them complete, he closed his eyes.

It was a moment or two before Isabel felt able to withdraw her fingers from where he'd discarded them. She felt awkward…chastised. Yet an apology clung to her throat. She knew he didn't want to hear it any more than he wanted her prying fingers on him. If they touched physically it would be on his terms only—to satisfy his lust. Other than that he had no need of her ministrations. He wanted no comfort or companionship. He had told her, had he not, that he had no desire to be her friend. He already had a lady friend of whom he was very fond. For the first time she felt a stab of jealousy for the woman who had her husband's love and respect.

She lay still and wondered if he had been cold while he slept, for the fingers that had captured her wrist had felt icy. He had retired fully clothed and it had not occurred to her to offer to share the quilt. Once Marcus was finished with the biscuits and off to sleep, they had sought their own rest with barely a word passing between them.

With a heavy heart she glanced towards the small window and noticed an impenetrable darkness behind the thin drapery. She guessed dawn to be fast approaching. With a sigh she burrowed without a perceptible movement into a warmer spot. As exhaustion again claimed her, her body instinctively curved towards the man beside her.

'How long will it be before we reach Suffolk?'

'About three weeks.'

Isabel's gaze darted from an uninspiring vista of undulating muddy brown fields. 'Three weeks?' Green eyes widened on her husband's face. 'Is that a joke? Why on earth will it take that long? We are travelling to Redgrave Park, surely?'

'I don't recall saying that we were heading there. We're going to London.' He sounded quite puzzled.

'You…you spoke of our home in Suffolk,' she argued excitedly. 'Yesterday you were telling Marcus about Redgrave Park.'

'Yes, I was. And we will go to Suffolk, but not just yet. I have important business to attend to in town. You must have known that my hasty marriage would result in problems. I have vital matters to attend to in the city before I can go home.'

'Yes, but…'

'I have a very comfortable house in Eaton Square. I keep it staffed and well equipped. You will have everything you need.'

'It is not that. I'm sure your house is more than adequate. I do understand that you have business to attend to, but first you must take Marcus and me to Suffolk. No, there is no need for you to accompany us. We can journey on alone, but you must provide us with transport. You may stay in Mayfair.'

'Thank you.' Her bold, breathless arrangements were met with an exceedingly dry response. 'Unfortunately I have no intention of allowing you to travel without me. We are all going to London and will remain there until I have dealt with every matter to my satisfaction.'

'I am not staying in London.'

'Don't be ridiculous.'

'I am *not* being ridiculous,' Isabel cried desperately.

'You are my wife and you will go where I do.' A fierce hooded look levelled at her. 'I believe you recently vowed to love, honour and obey. I accept the first two are unenforceable...' He didn't bother concluding the threat. Their eyes held combatively for a few seconds. At the same instant they became aware of their child's unusual stillness. Marcus was no longer regimenting his soldiers on the coach seat, but listening to their low-toned altercation with a grave solemnity.

Isabel's eyes swerved accusingly to her husband.

'I think we need to talk privately,' Etienne muttered bleakly. A clenched fist banged for the driver to halt. As the coach skidded to a shocked stop he flung open the door and was out before the wheels ceased turning. 'Stay there. We will only be a moment,' he told his son with quiet authority. Marcus slid himself back on the seat and neatly entwined his fingers, his hazel eyes poignantly watchful.

Etienne offered Isabel a hand and urged her immediately down, then was pacing at speed away from the coach, forcing his wife, her fingers imprisoned under his on his arm, to skip to keep up with him. The small spinney at the side of the road gave the seclusion necessary to evade the sidelong glances from Reeves and the coachman. A few yards into the shrubbery he came to an abrupt halt, making Isabel tilt back to avoid bumping into him.

'What in damnation is this all about?' The words were gritted and vibrant. Through a screen of denuded wood, he immediately peered at the coach as though to satisfy himself his son was not also being insubordinate and following them.

Isabel took a deep breath. She had hoped that this particular secret would not be necessarily revealed fast on the heels of the confession that her widowhood was a sham. She had hoped, in time, to bring a little dignity to the disclosure of her supposed demise. The idea that there might be a proper way to break such outrageous news almost wrung from her a hysterical laugh. As usual, when put on the defensive, she launched an attack. 'You will not bully me! Nor will you make me feel guilty about my wedding vows. How dare you be so hypocritical as to take *me* to task when you also blasphemed before the minister.'

'As I recall, that particular blasphemy was rather forced upon me.'

Isabel visibly winced. He would never let her forget that he was a reluctant partner in this marriage. 'No doubt your wedding to Miss Greenwood would have seen you uttering absolute truths about love and fidelity,' she snapped.

Etienne stared at her, then grimaced defeat. *'Touché,'* he muttered sardonically and stalked off a yard or so. 'Is this fit of temper prompted by what occurred between us last night?'

'I…it has nothing to do with what occurred last night. I have already forgotten about that.'

Etienne spun on a heel, raked her flushing face with piercing eyes. 'Have you indeed?' he said softly. 'I wish I could say the same.' He plunged his hands into his coat pockets. With his shoulders hunched he stared at bleak columns of bark. 'I apologise for acting like a drunken lout. I was angry with you, but the threats were empty. You had nothing to fear. I'm no more likely to violate you now than I was eight years ago. I'm sorry if I frightened you. I would have told you so earlier this morning, but an opportunity to be private didn't arise.'

The awkwardness and regret she read in his tense profile were emotions that were still bedevilling her. Being honest seemed only fair. 'I'm sorry too. I know I acted irrationally. What a stupid thing, believing you might have taken Marcus to the gypsies!' The hollow laugh withered in her throat. 'Let's not dwell on it, please.' She looked appealingly at him and he returned her a slanted smile.

'Nothing about this marriage is going to be easy, Isabel,' he told her quietly, reflectively. 'Every single day will be hard for I fear duty will never be quite enough for either of us.'

'I know.' Her agreement was little more than a sob.

'Why are you so set against going to London?'

'I…I cannot face the gossips. It is a long time since Rachel jilted Connor and I disappeared from society, but some people might enjoy resurrecting a mysterious scandal. I do not want Marcus exposed to the nastiness I know awaits us once our identities are discovered.' It was the truth, she thought, if not the whole truth.

'You are my wife and Marcus is my son. Do you think me so weak and ineffectual that I could not protect you from such malice? I know we have a mess to sort out and gossip to face. I will help you deal with it, I promise.'

'You don't understand,' Isabel said in a strangled voice. She looked off into trees, trying to find the words to explain. 'It is not just that people will be unkind. My family…my parents and my sisters…I have them to consider too. It is awkward…'

'You don't want to see them?'

'I want to see them very much, but I fear it is impossible.'

Etienne's eyes fixed on his wife's beautiful anxious face. Tears sparkled on her lashes in the weak early morning sunlight. Something stirred within him, something new that transcended masculine egotism in his vow to protect this courageous woman and their child. An urge to reach out and move her close, kiss and caress her was prompted by a desire to comfort rather than to assuage his lust. His hand involuntarily started to move towards her, was instead made into a fist and withdrawn. Any touch from him was likely to be met with suspicion. And after last night he couldn't blame her for that. He carefully thought over their predicament. 'Is there a secret you are holding back? Something I ought to know, but you are reluctant to tell me?'

Isabel gulped in a breath and nodded, thankful of his sharp perception.

'Well, we're halfway there, Isabel,' Etienne encouraged quietly. 'I know there is a problem, now all you must do is name it. Thereafter we can solve it.' He came close again, tilted up her downcast face with a single finger. 'Do you not trust me to put it right?'

'I trust you to try…but it is an insurmountable problem.'

'Let me be the judge of that,' he soothed, honey-voiced.

'Can you bring me back to life, Etienne? For in polite society I'm believed to be dead.'

Chapter Twelve

'Believed to be dead?' he echoed with a phantom smile in the words as though he thought her joking.

Isabel put a slender hand to her brow. A massaging thumb and forefinger bridged skin like alabaster. 'Let us return to the coach,' she breathed. 'Marcus will be fretting.'

'*I* am fretting,' he returned exceedingly quietly, a hand on her arm arresting her. 'Tell me a little more about your passing. Not so very long ago dismissing you as a figment of my imagination would have been most welcome. Now I'm not so sure. Lately I've appreciated having you around in the flesh.'

'It is not a matter for jest,' Isabel stormed. 'I am deadly serious. My parents did not anticipate my long absence would give rise to such rumours. It was no secret that I had accompanied Rachel when she jilted Connor and fled to York, or that a scarletina epidemic occurred whilst we were there. Rachel returned home to Hertfordshire, I did not. Sensitive people drew their own conclusions to my family's distress. Believing them bereaved, they let matters lie. Those who probed had their impertinence met with silence. My parents did not confirm or deny a single thing.'

'How very good of them. So the ruse of you being a widowed mother never circulated in the *ton?*'

Isabel shook her head 'There was no point in compounding the deceit unnecessarily. I knew I could never move back to Hertfordshire and blight my sisters' marriage prospects with a hint of scandal. But in York I needed to protect Aunt Florence's reputation for she would have been tainted with my shame. I assumed a respectable history and became Mrs Forrester. And there was Marcus… I couldn't bear the thought of him being branded a fatherless bast…' Completing the slur was impossible. 'I'm not sure the pretence was believed by all, but we were generally known as genteel, if shabby.'

'Did your father not properly support you during the time you lived with your aunt?'

High spots of colour rose on Isabel's cheeks at the blame in his tone. 'My papa has done enough for me...more than most would in the circumstances. I might have been welcomed home had I agreed to certain conditions. Papa sends bank drafts every so often.'

'When did you receive the last? How much was it for?' Etienne demanded.

Isabel bristled with filial loyalty. 'My parents have three other daughters, you know! At the time of Marcus's birth none were married. Rachel was thought to be on the shelf after jilting Connor. June was fifteen and soon due to make her come out, and Sylvie was just a child with her education *and* her début in front of her.' She listed her father's costly duties with a degree of proud indignation. 'There was much to be borne before he even began to think of weddings he must pay for and dowries he must settle on his three daughters.'

'He has four daughters,' Etienne reminded her. 'Did he consider buying *you* a husband somewhere out in the sticks? An indigent curate or the like?'

'Yes, he offered to do that.' She tipped up her chin revealing the fierce flush staining her throat. 'He also promised it was still possible I could return home to the bosom of my family, supposedly recovered at last from scarletina.'

'But you would not abandon Marcus.'

'No,' she replied simply, without emphasis or sanctimony. In a quick evading movement she was past him and striding out of the trees. It was not until she was sliding across the hide seat to instinctively, reassuringly gather her precious child to her that his warmth, seeping through her clothes, made her aware how chilled she was.

They had covered a few quiet miles before Isabel plucked up the courage to boldly ask, 'Will we arrive in Suffolk before nightfall?'

Before looking up, Etienne positioned his French general at the head of his army. Marcus commenced assassinating him with a battalion of English artillery, scattering tin figures over hide in the process. 'I cannot indulge you in this, Isabel.' His tone was mild, but his adamant refusal easily traversed Marcus's guttural gunfire. 'It is vital things are sorted out. The other business I have in town can wait. But I have a hankering to be introduced to your father as soon as possible.'

'What do you think on it all?'

'Mrs Drake don't let us gossip. Master don't like it. I don't think. I just do.'

'I reckon the nipper has a look of the Colonel about him. Give him a mop of dark hair and lovely brown eyes and he'd be a chip off the old block.'

'Shh…' Miriam Clarke put a work-rough finger against her lips. She flicked a duster at Felicity, the pretty young scullion who today had escaped the unpleasant heat of the kitchen due to a colleague's sickness and was promoted to assist above stairs. The two women were polishing fine yew furniture in the elegant drawing room of Number Forty-Nine Eaton Square. Miriam's eyes swivelled. Satisfied they were private, she easily relented to the urge to tattle. 'Little Master Marcus is a handsome lad. A heartbreaker in the making if ever I saw one.'

Felicity shot a sly look at her superior while tickling the top of a vase with feather tips. She had no wish to hurry through these duties and be relegated to the steamy bowels of the house. Rose-petal air spiced with beeswax polish was the sweetest perfume compared to the odour of cabbage water. 'The big master is a looker too and the one I'm better interested in. I'd say he's definitely a heartbreaker and lusty with it or I don't know me onions.'

'You don't want to let Mrs Drake hear you talk like that,' Miriam warned the newly recruited Felicity of the housekeeper's strict adherence to decorum and duty at this distinguished address. 'If she catches on you're getting above yourself, and you not here yet two whole weeks, you'll be back on the pavement sharpish. Best not let Mrs Hauke hear of it, neither. I know she looks a bit too refined to be bothered with the likes of saucy scullions; then again she might just smack your face for you. She's a bride, after all.'

Felicity clucked her indifference to the threats. 'I know what I'm doing and 'tain't scouring pots much longer, that's for sure.'

'You got more chance of warming Prinny's sheets!' Miriam scoffed. 'The Colonel's got a right swell ladybird to visit if his wife's indisposed. A proper beauty she is. Me and Jenkins saw her once in a grand carriage the master bought for her. A cabreelay, Jenkins says it is; he should know, 'cos he used to work in the coach house before he got his bad back. It's all shiny black paint with a silver crest and done out inside with silver cushions.' Miriam folded her arms across her chest, conscientiousness abandoned. 'She were dressed in silver-grey too, with her hair all done up and sleek as the black carriage horses. So dignified...'

'Grey cushions!' Felicity derided with her wrinkled nose joining up her freckles. The feather duster was let drop to the table. 'I'd want crimson; and gold wheels and white horses so everyone could see me coming.'

'That's 'cos you're common!' Miriam snorted. 'Lady Avery is a widow so she favours grey out of respect. She's a lady. She's refined.'

'Not *too* refined, though, is she?' Felicity sniped pointedly. 'Anyhow, when he's home she ain't available.' A suggestive wink accompanied that.

Miriam dismissed it with a hand flick. 'Mrs Hauke might not be a raving beauty, but she's got a look about her that's very nice. Anyhow, I reckon it's a love match.'

'Never! She's thin and pale with too much curly mousy hair. She must be a rich widow to get a man like him.'

Miriam pointed a warning finger. 'You'd best sheathe those claws, you cat. Colonel Hauke don't need another man's money. He's flush, he is. You're just jealous 'cos the Colonel's fallen for her.'

'Have you no work to do?'

Miriam and Felicity froze into twin statues: each with one hand on one jutting hip and chins aggressively jousting.

Isabel hadn't wanted to eavesdrop. Unfortunately, once she had gone into the anteroom to sit and quietly read while enjoying the last fading light to be had through the west window there was only one way out: past these two. She had hovered as dusk descended, hoping they would leave the room first and spare everyone's blushes. Finally, when their arguing began grating on her nerves, she had become annoyed enough at them, and at herself for feeling intimidated, to make her presence known. She now gave the petrified housemaids a cool assessing gaze. 'What are your names?'

'Miriam Clarke, ma'am,' the older woman gulped.

Isabel turned her attention to the younger servant. A raise of her finely shaped eyebrows elicited, 'Felicity Wright, ma'am.' It was ejected so feebly that Isabel barely caught the name. She felt her pique fading. The eager seductress looked little more than seventeen. She also appeared so ashen and terrified that Isabel feared she might swoon.

These two faces were vaguely familiar from when the staff had assembled to welcome her when she had arrived almost a week ago. Since then the only servants with whom she ever had regular dealings were Mrs Drake, the housekeeper, and the butler, Roland Forbes. The others she occasionally saw in passing. They had all treated her with due respect and deference...to her face.

Felicity Wright, then, was an ambitious scullion; had Isabel not heard it from her own lips she would have gleaned it from her appearance. She was the underling of the two women, yet her demeanour was superior. Her uniform was spruce and well fitting, her starched cap set at a jaunty angle on golden hair that was curled stylishly beneath it. 'How old are you, Felicity?' she asked quietly.

The maid's nervous tongue tip flicked at her lips. 'Sixteen, ma'am,' she croaked.

A sixteen-year-old temptress who had designs on her husband. As Isabel discreetly studied the comely young woman, she wondered how Etienne would react should Felicity succeed in letting him know.

'You both seem to be finished here.' Isabel deliberated on the idle dusting cloths and polish. 'I noticed a spillage has occurred on the floor close to the fire in the morning room. Perhaps my son's cordial was overset.'

'I'll see to it now,' Miriam garbled.

'I will too,' Felicity gasped and snatched up her duster so hastily rose petals were dislodged from overblown blooms and floated down to spatter shiny wood.

The ensuing stampede brought a twitch of a smile to Isabel's lips. 'Felicity, please stay a moment.'

The girl turned at the door, shocked. She cast one despondent look at Miriam. Her colleague refused to meet her eyes and slipped quickly away.

'Come here, please.' Isabel crooked a finger and reluctantly the scullion obeyed.

'How long have you been working here?'

'Two weeks, ma'am.'

'Speak up please, Felicity. Where did you work previously?'

'Lady Osborne's, ma'am, in Cavendish Square.'

'Were you a scullion in Cavendish Square?'

'No, ma'am. I was undermaid to Lady Osborne's maid.'

'Are you better suited to those duties?'

Felicity peeped warily through her lashes as though she believed it must be a trick question.

'Are you able to stitch neatly and dress a head of hair?' Isabel shortly persevered.

'Yes, ma'am, when I worked for Lady Osborne I did embroidery and hair styling. Lady Osborne's maid was training me up to work for Lady Catherine, Lady Osborne's daughter. I liked it.'

'Why did you leave? Were you unhappy there?'

Felicity looked confused and remained silent.

'Did Lady Osborne give you a character?'

The girl looked uneasy. 'No, ma'am,' she croaked.

'Why not?'

Felicity blushed and her lips wobbled. ''Cos…'cos I was put off when her son took particular notice of me.'

'I see. And that is why you have been taken on scouring pans here? Because you had no character to give Mrs Drake?'

The girl nodded miserably.

'Well, I have need of a lady's maid and I would rather train someone to do things my way. I always use my own herbal preparations. Would you be interested in helping to prepare lotions and so on?'

'I would…yes…' Felicity resonantly stressed.

'I shall speak to Mrs Drake then about your change in duties. That is all. You may go.'

'Thank you, ma'am,' Felicity garbled. She hovered close by the door and Isabel knew the girl was trying to find a way to apologise for her audacious personal attack. They both knew her comments had been overheard. 'You may go, Felicity,' Isabel directed firmly for she had no wish to be reminded of them.

Isabel dredged the scattered petals into a fist. She wandered to the half-open window and let them fall to the terrace flags. Despite her desire to forget the gossips, her imagination would not allow her peace. It was surprising how servants' opinions veered between the mundane and the fascinating. Odd, too, that one could feel flattered or humiliated by the observations of people deemed to be of little consequence. Isabel took a silky spiralling curl and brought it into her line of vision. It was definitely *not* mousy. She'd always liked her hair's unusual shade of fair.

The maidservants' gossip was not all news to her. She already knew her husband kept a mistress; he'd freely disclosed that information himself. But Miriam and Felicity had coloured the sketchy image she had in her mind of a woman Etienne might love. She now knew his good friend was a titled lady and that he had provided her with a luxurious cabriolet carriage upholstered in silver to compliment her shiny black hair and penchant for grey gowns. Lady Avery was deemed refined. Little wonder her husband was besotted with such a paragon, Isabel thought with a wry smile.

As for Felicity wanting to improve her status, there was nothing novel in a maidservant's aspiration to climb out of the kitchens and into the master's bed. Similar shenanigans occurred in households throughout the land. What *was* peculiar was the master's wife providing the interloper with an opportunity to get a foot on the stairs. Why had she just promoted Felicity to a position where she was likely to frequently encounter the object of her desire?

A poignant ache within provided her answer and it was an insight she would rather ignore. Malice had prodded her into action, she realised. Felicity Wright, pretty as she was, would always be less important to Etienne than his love. But Lady Avery might have her power diluted by an eager rival. With a stab of anguish Isabel realised she resented the woman's grip on Etienne. And that was a terrifying thing. She didn't want to care. She didn't want to want him…ever again. She had married him to provide a decent future for their son, not to try and wrest his affection from the woman he loved.

Since their arrival in town Isabel had realised just how strong was his bond with his mistress. He was rarely at home. Sometimes he did not even return for dinner in the evening and she dined alone with Marcus. At night his chamber, connected to hers by a dressing room, was invariably quiet enough to be unoccupied.

She had nothing of which to accuse him. Their every comfort was met. He had made it clear she could purchase what she liked: furniture for the house, clothes for herself or their son. A substantial allowance was available to her should she wish to make visits or outings. She had thanked him politely for his generosity and refrained from reminding him that she had no friends here and no need of new gowns in which to socialise at home...alone.

She had never visited Suffolk, but yearned to move to that unknown county as soon as possible. She therefore did not have the heart or interest to replace furniture in his Mayfair townhouse that, in any case, was of the finest quality and taste.

The sound of the front door closing shattered her poignant introspection. Her stomach clenched in something akin to excitement and that made her tremble. She didn't want her husband's arrival home to affect her in such a way. She didn't want to find herself listening for the key in the lock. Nevertheless, she could not prevent her hands going to automatically check her dress and hair as she emerged into the corridor of his gracious house. She ran an appreciative eye over the fine paintings, the carved plasterwork and sombre oak doors as she walked towards the vestibule. She was lonely without Rachel and her friends in Ireland, she told herself as her pace quickened. It was the reason for her eagerness to have a little adult company every so often. It wasn't specifically *him* she wanted to see. Yet she had found that, when he bestowed his time, she could enjoy their conversations.

'Is Colonel Hauke home?' she needlessly asked Roland Forbes. She could tell from the greatcoat and cane he was carrying to the cloaks cupboard that he indeed had returned.

'He is, madam. I believe he went off toward his study,' Roland told her with a kind smile.

Isabel hesitated with a hand raised to knock. She let it drop to her side and with a deep breath walked in, unannounced.

Etienne was standing with his back to her, close to the smouldering coals in the grate. His dark head was bent towards the mantel; so lost in thought did he appear to be that he did not even turn at the sound of her arrival.

'Am I disturbing you?' She hated sounding so timid. To make amends she said more firmly, 'I just wondered if you would be home for dinner this evening. I wondered whether to wait…or dine earlier with Marcus.'

'Are you asking me to stay home for dinner this evening?' He turned slowly to look at her.

Isabel returned his stare, taken aback. She had not anticipated he might say that. She searched his handsome face with eyes that were soulful. *Yes…* whispered in her mind. Aloud she said briskly, 'No. But there are important things we ought to talk over and as you are rarely home during the day…or night…'

That waspish observation elicited a half-smile. 'You sound as though you've missed me, Isabel,' he said with soft mockery. 'Have you?'

Isabel felt her face getting hot. She wondered whether he had spent this afternoon with Lady Avery; shopping with her, perhaps, or driving with her in her smart carriage with silver cushions. 'I imagine I've missed you as much as you've missed me,' she countered with an admirably insouciant smile.

'And that sounds as though you'd like to know whether I have missed you. Would you?'

'No,' Isabel lied quickly. 'But I would like to know whether you have missed your son, for he is always looking for you.'

'Well, I'm certainly aware when he's not around,' Etienne returned ironically, but his tone was not unkind.

'He can be rather...boisterous,' Isabel admitted on a twist of a smile.

'So could I at that age. Thank you for the invitation to dine with you. I accept.'

Isabel opened her mouth to retort that it was not an invitation, but the humorous look in his eyes kept her silent. He had anticipated a rebuff. 'We ought to talk about our move to Suffolk and how Marcus is dealing with his new tutor. Mr Barton seems efficient but rather…rather blunt in his manner.'

'I understand, Isabel,' he said quietly. 'You want me for the problems and practicalities only. I understand that…'

Isabel dropped her eyes. After a pause she ventured, 'I'm sorry if that seems selfish to you…'

A hoarse laugh erupted and he turned and stabbed a toe at the fender. 'Selfish? No. Vengeful? Yes. But as we're civilised now you'll keep your vengeance gentle, I know. I don't anticipate any more obvious battle wounds.' He abruptly pulled a decanter close and tipped a shot into a glass. 'Dinner is at eight, I believe?'

She was being dismissed, Isabel realised. She backed away a few paces, her chin high. 'Yes, it is. Please don't be late. Marcus will be hungry,' was all she said as she closed the door.

Chapter Thirteen

'I have appointed a lady's maid from amongst your servants.'

'Good.'

'Her name is Felicity Wright,' Isabel informed him casually.

Knowing the identity of the young woman altered her husband's expression not one jot.

'She is young but quite bright and ambitious…and pretty.'

Etienne lifted his glass to his lips. 'She sounds deserving of promotion,' he remarked conversationally, but without any indication he recognised the person under discussion. 'What were her duties previously?'

'Scouring pots and pans.'

Etienne replaced his wine untasted. A frowning smile flickered over the candelabra gleaming midway between them on the dining table. He obviously understood enough of the female servants' hierarchy to know such an elevation was extraordinary.

'She arrived here without a character. Lady Osborne put her off,' Isabel quickly explained.

Etienne's bemusement increased. 'Are we taking on waifs and strays now?' He paused to lounge back in his chair. 'Earlier in the week Marcus had a son of one of the grooms in his bedchamber, sorting through soldiers. Today he had two more scruffy young scamps I've never before seen playing chase in the garden.'

'Yes, I know,' Isabel said. 'I told them all they were very welcome to play. They are polite children. It is good Marcus has friends.'

Etienne picked up his wine goblet, twirled it in his fingers while looking reflectively into ruby ripples. 'I agree. But do you not think he ought be socialising with children of his own class?'

'What class is that, pray?' Isabel asked quietly.

Beneath lowered brows Etienne's dark eyes slanted to hers. 'It is a class that befits his new station in life as my son and intended heir. He is my natural, first-born son. I have every intention of securing the succession for him. If he succeeds to an earldom he will probably also take a viscountcy, if my Uncle Archibald dies without issue. As he is now sixty-one and has never shown the remotest interest in women or marriage, I imagine that will be the case.'

Seizing a change of subject, Isabel asked on a nervous laugh, 'Does your uncle not like women?'

'He prefers men.'

At this blunt statement Isabel frowned in consideration, then blushed. 'Oh, I see.'

'My uncle's predilection for lifelong bachelorhood spurred my father to marry too young and too soon: he wanted to reassure his father that he was not of the same persuasion. My grandfather was also keen for the ultimate *mésalliance*,' he remarked with dark irony. 'He wanted his younger son to provide him with grandchildren, as the heir apparent was unlikely to continue the line. My grandfather successfully fought to secure the earldom for my father and his descendants on his death. He had no intention of expiring and allowing Archie to inherit. He is convinced his detested heir will see out his century. My grandfather and uncle haven't spoken for more than forty years.'

To spare her further blushes at this highly improper information, Isabel reverted to discussing their son. 'Marcus would also like his friend Michael Murphy, from Waterford, to come and visit him once we are settled in Suffolk. Would you object to me writing and asking his parents' permission?'

'When he gets to school, Marcus shall make friends amongst his peers,' Etienne returned evenly.

At the oblique refusal Isabel picked up her wineglass. 'Of course... I had forgotten how very high and mighty you are.'

'How foolish of you,' her husband said, impenitent. 'Now, tell me why it appears I am taking in Lady Osborne's castoffs. The maid you mentioned earlier is acceptable here, but not there? Why?'

'It's true she was taken on without a character and put scouring pans,' Isabel confirmed slowly while her mind quickly sought a justification for that peculiarity. 'I expect Mrs Drake noticed her worth. Beneath that stern exterior I think your housekeeper is fair and wise and she has recognised that Felicity is sharp and smart.'

'Sharp and smart enough to be caught pilfering from Lady Osborne?'

'No. It wasn't that.' Isabel leapt to her new maid's defence. Felicity was showing great promise and very real humility for having spoken with such saucy impudence of her master and mistress. 'She isn't a thief. Lady Osborne's son took a particular interest in her, that's all.' The realisation that she was unwittingly digging a deeper hole for poor Felicity to tip into left her busily attending to her dinner.

'*That's all?* For Heaven's sake!' Etienne's groan was followed by a bark of laughter prompted by sheer disbelief. His wine goblet found the table with a thump. 'And no doubt her bastard will be coddled in my household or I'll again be accused of being high and mighty.'

Isabel stared at her plate and sighed softly. 'No, I don't think we need worry over…that.'

Etienne's sardonic amusement softened; his eyes became warm and intense. He inclined towards her, resting his elbows on the table. 'It hadn't occurred to you that perhaps we should, had it? And that surprises me,' he added, velvet-voiced. 'Considering our circumstances and your history, I imagined you were already feeling empathetic and destined to help the poor ruined maid. You really are an innocent, aren't you?'

'She isn't ruined and you don't need to mock me so.'

'I'm not mocking you, Isabel,' her husband said with husky sincerity. 'Truth be known, I'm humbled by the way you've coped alone for so long. I admire you…in lots of ways…'

'I've not coped alone. I have had help from my relations.' Isabel championed the Merediths while challengingly holding his gaze. 'Are you drunk?' She eyed his empty wine glass with suspicion.

'No, I'm not drunk. Do I need to be drunk to pay my wife a compliment?' He pushed back his chair and stood up, sleepy-eyed and purposeful.

Isabel stood too. He looked groomed to perfection and heartbreakingly handsome, resplendent in close-fitting fawn breeches and black tailcoat. In his snow-white neckcloth winked a sizeable emerald. He looked ready for an evening abroad. He looked like a gentleman with an important assignation. 'Are you going out?' Isabel demanded in a tone that couldn't quite conceal her disappointment at the likelihood.

'No, I'm not going out.' Etienne ceased stalking her. 'Are you?' The irony in his tone told her he had noticed the way she was instinctively retreating towards the door.

'Me? Going out? Where would I go? *I* don't have a special friend to visit.' The thoughts dogging her mind were involuntarily voiced and she turned away from him, mortified. 'I'm sorry, I shouldn't have said that. Forget I said that, please.'

'I don't want to forget you said it. I'm pleased you're jealous. But there is no need to be.'

'I am *not* jealous,' Isabel stormed, furious that he had sensed the emotion tormenting her. She didn't want to acknowledge its existence; she certainly didn't want *him* to know Lady Avery bothered her.

'Do you want to know why I've been absent from home so often since we arrived in London?'

'I've no interest in what you do socially,' she lied. 'When we struck our bargain I expected no more than your discretion in a token marriage, I told you that.'

'And now?'

'And now I have no complaints,' Isabel stated in a proud, husky voice.

'Well, I have,' Etienne told her quietly. 'We're dining together, talking together about children and servants. We're doing natural things married people do. You welcome me now because you need me. I need you too, Isabel. There are other natural things married people do…' His words tailed off and his eyes slid past and narrowed on the door.

Isabel watched his lips form a soundless curse and five fingers wreak havoc on his neatly combed long hair. He strode to the mantel and braced a weathered hand against it. His focus was now the highly polished boot he'd jammed on the fender.

As the draught from the door whispered into her silken skirts Isabel whipped about with an inkling of the reason for her husband's barely concealed irritation. 'You should be abed, Marcus!' she softly chided her son loitering on the threshold.

Marcus wrinkled his nose, gathered his dressing gown away from his feet and padded closer. Brightly he declared, 'I'm not tired. I'm still hungry.'

'How can you be hungry?' Etienne demanded in a blast of frustration. 'When you left the table you were full. That was barely an hour ago. Now off to bed with you this instant! Your mama and I have things we must talk about in private.'

Marcus stared, shocked and unblinking, at his father. His lower lip began to wobble before it was thrust defiantly.

Isabel raised appealing eyes to Etienne. 'Don't shout at him please, it never helps. He…he…'

'He is spoiled; he is in need of heeding some rules,' Etienne supplied with soft steel.

'He is not spoiled.' Isabel moistened her lips, then allowed softly, 'He is…wilful, I know, but that is not entirely his fault.'

'No, it's mostly my fault,' Etienne accepted quietly. 'And I'll rectify it. Go back to bed now,' he directed his son with absolute calm authority. 'If you do not, your friends will not be allowed to come here and play and your friend in Ireland will not be allowed to visit Redgrave Park.'

'I don't care!' Marcus burst out belligerently. His large eyes skipped warily from his father's harsh forbidding countenance to seek reassurance from his gentle mama.

Isabel quickly blinked away the heat in her eyes and held out a hand to her beloved burden. 'Come, I'll take you back to bed.'

'Marcus found his way here on his own. He can similarly find the way back,' Etienne stated in a perilously mild voice. 'He is, after all, a boy of seven years old, not a baby in leading strings. He is not infirm and has no need to be taken about by the hand.'

'I'm not a baby, Mama,' Marcus bravely echoed his father's words. 'I can go on my own back to bed.' After a few moments standing there poignantly uncertain, he retreated a step, then another until he was again in the hall.

'How dare you!' Isabel choked when the door was closed. 'How dare you criticise *me* over the way I have reared him...cared for him.'

'When did I do that?' her husband asked, his anger tightly controlled.

'*When?* All the time! Not blatantly, perhaps, but there is a hint of disapproval in every look, every word you direct his way. I'm sure you enjoy finding fault with him,' she cried.

'That is not true, Isabel, and you know it.'

'It is true!' she insisted. 'You may despise me if you like, but you ought have the decency to fairly treat an innocent child. But why should you care for his feelings?' she choked through a coagulation of tears in her throat. 'You don't love him; you don't even like him. You resent giving him your name and I don't believe you will endeavour to make him your legitimate heir. To you he will always be the brat who was foisted on to you by that scheming harlot you once—'

Through a misty blur Isabel saw he was getting closer. The heel of a palm smeared the wet from her eyes. She had again said too much and made herself appear hysterical and foolish. Swiftly she shook back her rebellious curls from her smudged face, then swished about and made for the door. Before she had opened it an inch a hand slammed across her shoulder, shutting it again.

'You might be finished, my dear, but I am not. Don't run off just as things are getting interesting. Refresh my memory over this scheming harlot, for I'm damned if I can recall much about her...yet I'd like to.'

Isabel whipped about and flattened against the door. Her glistening green eyes raked his hard face. Despite his anger sultry desire was radiating from between long black lashes, bathing her in feverish heat. 'That's all you're interested in, isn't it? Getting your reward for marrying me and providing for my son. I agreed to the bargain; you need not fear I will renege and beg you not to,' she breathed contemptuously up at him. 'You want your pound of flesh so much. Have it! Now!' She ripped at the buttons on her dress with trembling fingers. The bodice gaped, her small, lush bosom visible over a froth of lace on her chemise. She went on to tiptoe, furiously slammed her mouth onto his, and ground her soft salty lips against the cool inflexibility of his while fresh tears slid between them.

A hand delved into her honey hair, winding a silky hank about a broad palm. Slowly, as though the denial was an ordeal, her mouth was moved back from his. 'If I was desperate, perhaps I would. But you know I'm not. I've been seduced with more finesse, Isabel, lots of times. Even by scheming harlots.' The words were flippant, taunting but he couldn't quite discipline his yearning eyes from ravening her delectable swollen flesh, pure and fine as alabaster. A hand hovered by her throat before just one long finger, slightly unsteady, lowered to trace the valley between her silken breasts.

Isabel gasped an involuntarily shuddering breath at the exquisite sensation, and dusky pink crescents peeped over a snowy filigree to tease him.

Within an instant he had swung her away from the door and deposited her on the nearest armchair with a speed that indicated a vehement need to be distanced from her. Isabel grasped at the arms to prevent sliding to the floor.

The dishevelled picture of wanton womanhood she presented, with her clothing awry and her mermaid hair trailing her naked pearly shoulders, brought dull slashes of heat to highlight Etienne's cheekbones. With a savage curse, that he this time made no attempt to modulate in volume, he turned his back on her. A hand went to the inside pocket of his jacket and a letter was extracted in a savage rip. 'Here; the reason why I've been away from home so often.' He pivoted on a heel and the letter was skimmed at her, landing on the rug by her feet. 'I've been tracking your father between Hertfordshire and Mayfair. He quit London just before we arrived. When I reached Hertfordshire I was informed by the staff at Windrush that your parents had set out for Berkshire to visit your sister, Sylvie. She's a pupil at an academy there. I left a message with your father's steward at Windrush. This is his reply. Your parents are due to arrive in London tomorrow and are coming to visit us at three in the afternoon. I'll endeavour to be home by then.'

'Is Etienne coming back?'
'I expect so, Marcus. Come here; let me

straighten your waistcoat. You will not want to meet your grandpapa and grandmama looking untidy.'

'I wish Etienne was here. I don't want to see these relations people. They don't like me. Is Etienne cross with me? Does *he* like me?' Marcus asked his mother anxiously as he succumbed to her ministrations. He stood obligingly still while she tucked in his shirt and fastened small pearl buttons on his blue waistcoat.

'Yes, of course.' She gave her son a reassuring smile and went to the window for what seemed like the hundredth time. It was almost two o'clock in the afternoon and she had not seen her husband since he had departed yesterday. The dining-room door and the front door had been slammed in quick succession and with such force that the noise had reverberated around the marble vestibule, bringing Roland Forbes to investigate the din. She was thankful she had had the sense to straighten her clothing before the butler appeared. Kindly he had insisted on fetching her a warm drink to take to bed before he tactfully withdrew, sorrowfully shaking his head to himself.

So now the servants also knew they were at loggerheads. They had parted on awful terms, but would Etienne still be so angry that he would punish her by letting her face her family alone? Was he capable of such incivility? She pushed the curtain back into place, increasingly agitated. The prospect of an audience with her parents was so nerve-racking that she hoped Etienne would reappear just so she could castigate him for having arranged it. Yet she knew it to be a vital meeting and less daunting than other confrontations that were sure to ambush her on the rocky road of her return to society.

On impulse she approached a writing desk. Her frantic fingers scrabbled the recesses for a pen and parchment while she fretted over the wisdom of despatching a note to Beaulieu Gardens, her parents' London residence, postponing their visit.

'If Etienne comes back I'll be good…I will. I won't get out of bed again. I won't be bad…'

'Well, that's good news.' A hint of gruff irony was in the praise.

'Etienne!' Marcus rushed to embrace his father about the knees.

Etienne looked down at a rapt upturned face. Abruptly he lifted his son and imperceptibly skimmed his fair hair with his lips. 'What did we agree you must call me now?' he asked softly.

Marcus raised his laughing eyes. 'Papa.'

'Yes. Papa. Have you been good this morning for your mama?'

Marcus looked thoughtful, then nodded quickly.

Putting him back on the carpet, Etienne walked over to where his wife sat. Her nervous fingers dropped the pen she still had poised over parchment.

Isabel suddenly got to her feet. 'I don't want to see them. I was about to write and tell them so.'

'Yes, you do want to see them.' Etienne corrected softly, a hand light on her arm, arresting her flight.

Isabel raised her eyes to his, losing herself in the velvet depths of his regret until she realised it was very probable his tardiness was due to the fact he had only lately torn himself away from his mistress.

As though reading her thoughts exactly, Etienne said, 'I made the acquaintance of an agreeable gentleman at my club. William Pemberton is by all accounts married to your sister June. I stayed there last night.'

'With June and her husband at Richmond?' Isabel's astonishment was plain in her voice.

'No. At White's.'

'Well, I'm sure *William* did not. He and June are *happily* married.'

Etienne allowed a sardonic quirk to tilt his lips at the inference in that. 'Yes, he told me so...many times. He seems a contented man. I envy him. But he did stay at White's. I'm not sure why.'

This information rather took the gale out of her sails. She had always got on well with her sister June. 'I haven't seen June since their marriage,' she said nostalgically. 'I was not invited to attend, of course. But shortly after their honeymoon they came to secretly visit us at Aunt Florence's. They kindly brought Marcus a present: the soldiers he plays with all the time. I don't expect he would remember his aunt and uncle. It was almost two years ago that they were married.'

'Well, they are eager to see Marcus again; you too. I had to dissuade your brother-in-law from dashing home to fetch his wife and calling on us immediately. They are visiting us tomorrow.'

'I'm not sure I want to see any of them. It's been so long…'

'You need to be reconciled with your parents and your sisters. It is the first step back into the land of the living, Isabel.' Her husband smiled wryly. 'I've no intention of letting you hide away. Rumours might start that I have shut my bride away in the attic, never to see the light of day,' he gently teased. 'I'm not ashamed of you and I won't have people think that I am. In fact, I'm proud of you both.'

He sounded sincere and Isabel yearned to believe him. But so much bitterness and betrayal lay between them. Niggling doubts persisted about his motives. Was it self-interest? She didn't think Etienne Hauke was a man who would take kindly to being mocked or pitied. He would want his wife and his son to be a credit to him and accepted by the *ton*. Perhaps he was determined to mould Marcus and her into characters worthy of the privileges soon to be bestowed by an earldom.

Etienne watched her face, and knew from her quiet introspection that the truths he had humbly tendered were met with cynicism. He could hardly blame her for being sceptical considering the turmoil they had been through. 'We must have in place a plausible story to outwit the scandalmongers.' A rueful smile preceded, 'I'm afraid we must do more than simply explain ourselves to friends and relatives. There are those people who are neither, who will relish shredding your reputation…mine too. So, we must socialise for a short while just to confound the gossips with our shameless unconcern.'

At the look of apprehension on her face, he smoothed his hand soothingly against her cheek. 'You can do it. It is the only way to win, Isabel: to broadcast our own version of events in the hope of stealing a march and deflating the windbags. There need not be a major scandal if we provide them with a minor one of our own choosing.'

Chapter Fourteen

'What sort of scandal?'

Etienne slanted a significant glance at their son. 'Why do you not fetch your soldiers, Marcus? I'm sure your grandpapa might like to see them. He will be here soon with your grandmama.'

Once the boy was from the room he continued without preamble. 'You have been in exile for many years. During that time you could have been anywhere. The last that was commonly known of your whereabouts was that you travelled to York with Rachel when she jilted Connor. It was no secret that a day or so later I went there too, although my purpose was kept private. That much of our history is real. Thereafter we must romanticise a bit.'

Etienne found himself drowning in the twin green pools of a serene gaze. How trusting she looked when she needed him.

'In York, we met by chance and fell in love at first sight,' he continued calmly and then expended a moment wondering where was the sarcastic laugh he had intended should accompany the myth. He forged on, 'Although we were virtual strangers we eloped, intending to be married as soon as possible, but there was no time for a wedding in England as I was called back to my regiment to give evidence at a court-martial.' The spinning of the yarn was broken for him to interject, 'It is the truth. After I arrived at my grandfather's house in Cambridge, I received a message almost immediately ordering my return overseas.'

'It is as well there are some actual facts,' Isabel remarked, intrigued by the weaving of the fabrication. She nodded at him to continue.

'You accompanied me to Belgium, prepared to follow the drum for my sake and it was there I seduced you. In the chaos preceding Waterloo we were separated and you scraped by, helped by fellow soldiers' consorts. Some months later you heard I had been taken prisoner behind enemy lines and executed by the French. You managed to get a passage home where you lodged with your Aunt Florence in

York and gave birth to our son a short time later.'

'But you were a prisoner of war before we met, not after.' Isabel interrupted to point out the discrepancy.

Etienne chuckled softly. 'I know that and you know that, but we must hope that people don't bother referencing dates. So long as a thread of truth runs through it all I'm hoping our audience will be dumbfounded by the quixotic nature of it all. Besides, it is all in the past. Now you are a perfectly respectable married lady you will probably be fêted for your magnificent courage in risking all for love.' He concluded the tale with an optimistic smile. 'Meanwhile I escaped my French gaoler and was distraught to hear a tale that the vessel you had been aboard, en route to England, had foundered in a storm. Thus we both believed the other perished.' Noting Isabel's dubious frown, he reassured her, 'It is only comparatively recently that a chance meeting between us has been likely. Although my friend and your sister have been wed almost two years, it is the first opportunity I have had to visit them at Wolverton Manor. From that point we can revert to the truth. It was at their home in Ireland that we renewed our acquaintance, falling in love all over again, and immediately getting wed. A fitting ending to the epic.'

Isabel gave a sour laugh. 'I applaud your vivid imagination. The finale is a great work of fiction, apart from the fact that we did meet again and get married.'

'As I said before,' he murmured, 'the calendar is slightly out; nevertheless, there's truth in it, Isabel.'

'Mr and Mrs Meredith are arrived, sir,' Roland Forbes announced into a still silence.

Etienne took his wife's small, unsteady fingers, pressed them to his warm lips before drawing them through his arm. He turned her about to face the door. 'Please show them in, Forbes.'

Isabel felt stunned; her parents' arrival was almost incidental as her mind dwelled on what her husband had just implied. Was he saying he loved her? Or was he simply boosting her courage with flattery? She took a quick glance up at his impassive profile. Perhaps he arrogantly believed that she was still yearning for him. A poignant feeling stirred. As he'd confidently declared, there was truth in it...

Any further private talk was impossible. Marcus was trotting back in to the room with an overflowing armful of tin. Edgar Meredith was behind him, stooping creakily at intervals to retrieve those clattering soldiers scattering in his grandson's wake.

Of a sudden four voices were disjointedly mingling without any proper preliminaries having taken place.

'Here, you dropped these, young man.'

'Are you my grandpapa?'

'Bella...oh, Bella! How well you look! How beautiful...' Gloria Meredith gushed, her voice so overflowing with tears that her daughter's frozen heart melted.

'Mama...' Swiftly Isabel slipped her hand from beneath her husband's possession and glided across the carpet to her mother. After an infinitesimal hesitation in which dear features were devoured, they clung, dipped heads concealing dewy eyes.

'This one is my favourite,' Marcus announced to his grandfather, thrusting a figure towards a grizzled face. 'He looks like my papa. Isn't he fierce? So is his horse. That's Storm, you know.'

'Hmm, I see, yes,' Edgar Meredith mumbled with a squint at a featureless cavalry officer brandishing a lance and mounted on a sinewy destrier. He took a peer at the flesh-and-blood model detachedly watching the proceedings.

Etienne squarely met that appraising glance. He strolled forward and offered a hand. 'I must thank you for responding quickly to my letter. I'm pleased to meet you, sir. There is much we have to say to one another.'

Edgar Meredith straightened to his full height, bringing him just short of Etienne's shoulders. The older man looked up coolly at his host before extending a hand and gamely challenging his grip. 'Indeed, there is much needs to be said,' he agreed, but with an air of pious condescension. 'Nevertheless, I'm pleased to meet *you* at last and overjoyed to find my daughter and grandson are finally re-spectable.' A sentimental look slanted at his wife and daughter conversing in low intimate tones.

Isabel led her mother towards a chair then went to the bell pull, announcing, in her first role as hostess, that they must all have tea. Gloria Meredith was soon up out of the comfy seat and bending down close to her grandson. One of her plump, elegantly bejewelled hands went to cup his fair face. She studied him with adoring eyes as he held up more soldiers for her to inspect.

'Etie…my papa,' Marcus corrected himself with a shy smile for his vigilant father. 'My papa said you might like to play soldiers.'

'I would indeed,' his grandmother agreed and, settling herself on a settee, she ranged her infantry alongside her satin skirts.

Edgar glanced at his besotted wife and his eyes became misty. 'It is a tragedy to have been deprived of our daughter and grandson for so long. But I like to think I don't bear grudges,' he ended briskly. 'I know it was not *all* your fault. Isabel admitted as much. And now things are come right at last, you need not fear we will be cold to you.'

'I think it best we leave our wives to get to know each other again while we talk in private. Would you care to accompany me to my study so that we might be properly introduced?' Etienne barely waited for his father-in-law's nod before he excused them both and headed for the door.

Once buffered within his darkly carved and panelled den, Etienne gestured his hospitality at his guest with a crystal glass and decanter.

Edgar accepted and was soon in possession of a fine goblet holding a generous measure of Madeira. After a silent few minutes, in which he began to shift uneasily beneath his new son-in-law's ruthless regard, Edgar rumbled, 'Hmm, well, it's not too late for you to make amends to all concerned. I've heard from my eldest daughter, Rachel, that the boy can be a mite mischievous. But he is young enough to be corrected. I'm sure you are sorry to have abandoned and neglected your own flesh and blood.'

'Indeed. But then I was ignorant of Marcus's existence. What is your excuse?' Etienne enquired with deadly quiet.

Startled, Edgar dropped his glass away from his desiccated lips. 'What?'

'You heard me. I asked, what is your excuse for neglecting your own flesh and blood?'

'How dare you, sir, accuse *me!*'

'Very easily do I accuse you,' Etienne bit out silkily. 'How generous has been your financial help to Isabel over those years? Why have you not taken it upon yourself to arrange a proper education at a decent school for your grandson?'

Edgar thumped down his drink on a table, slopping wine over a polished surface. 'My Jezebel daughter is fortunate she has parents who still acknowledge her!' he roared so violently that the whole of his small frame quivered. 'Were we not so devoted we might have cast her off with not two halfpennies to rub together to keep warm her and her bastard. For more years than I cared to countenance I met the cost of a modest keep for them with my wife's widowed sister, Florence.' A mottled hand swiped irate foam away from his mouth before he resumed his tirade. 'Would you have had me keep the hussy in equal style to her virtuous sisters at home? When the disaster occurred I did everything in my power to try and persuade the little fool to see sense and give up the boy. I found a couple willing to shelter him in amongst their brood. Money changed hands—an inducement for them to take him—

and was lost to their avarice when Isabel refused to let him go.'

'But you deemed these people suitable foster-parents for your grandson,' Etienne mentioned with such icy calm that Edgar blanched.

'Don't dare moralise to me, sir! Where were *you* in all this? *I* wanted to help give Isabel a decent future after you ruined her. It would have been simple enough to blame the epidemic in York for her lengthy absence. I would have welcomed her home with open arms had she seemed remorseful and unlikely to corrupt her sisters. But try as I might to persuade her, she wouldn't give up her child, or show proper penitence for disgracing us. None of our daughters were then married, nor ever would have been had the extent of the scandal leaked out.' Edgar's complexion became ruddy with blotches and blood vessels as vainly he attempted to govern his swingeing ire. 'Now you dare to find *me* wanting in this disaster of *your* making?' he exploded. 'You want to bring *me* to book for not paying for *your* son's education?'

With the exasperation of a man who knows history will not be reformed, no matter what money or curses he throws at it, Etienne bawled, 'Why in hell did you never try to find me?'

'Find you?' Edgar scoffed in an equal bellow. 'How was *I* to find you? *She* knew little enough about you, so she insisted. I think she knew more than she let on, but was afraid I might just have you tracked and horsewhipped. The little fool was under the impression you would soon return of your own volition to claim her. And I could not disabuse her of that innocent opinion, no matter how often I lectured on the ways of men and the wicked world. I had found a tempting dowry and a husband who would get her to the altar before the child was born. He was an inoffensive bookkeeper in his middle years, living with his widowed mother in a village north of Windrush. It was close enough for us all to keep in touch. She refused him. I think even when the babe was mewling in her arms, she still fantasised of happy endings. She believed that you would come back.'

Edgar barely paused for breath before rattling on in a seething tone, '*And* you need not think that we are yet free from the taint of it all. We must yet brave the gossips. What fun they will have.' Edgar took a stomp about the room, returning to stand and march with his back to the warm grate.

'Harry Greenwood is a vexed man. The dragon he is married to is breathing fire. By all accounts you led them to believe you would offer for *their* chit, Caroline. I've not had the nerve to let on that it's *my* chit you've married.'

'Nothing was formally agreed. I have already made my apologies to the Greenwoods. I have to say Miss Greenwood was less concerned than her mother that I would not be paying further addresses to her. Harry is resigned to it all. We have some other business of mutual benefit arranged.'

'Ha! That won't quieten his lady. You'll need St George for that! *And* she is friendly with my sister and my daughter June's mother-in-law, Pamela Pemberton. It don't bear thinking about. What I want to know is, what are we to *say* about it all?'

Etienne smiled with trenchant irony. 'If I can slide a few words in, I shall be happy to oblige you with that information.'

Once Etienne had recounted the mitigating circumstances concocted from truth and falsehood, Edgar seemed a mite mollified. It wasn't just the charming ruse that explained away his daughter's scandalously overdue marriage to the father of her child that pleased him. He recognised, beneath his son-in-law's bellicose exterior, a man who was fundamentally decent.

Etienne Hauke had had no need to marry Isabel or formally take on his illegitimate son. He could have made discreet provision for them before again burying them in his past. It was the usual way affluent gentlemen disposed of such unforeseen aberrations from their youth.

When Edgar had received the fellow's confessional letter his first reaction had been astonishment that, after so many years elapsed between the passion and the present, the knave even owned up to the deed. To volunteer to accept such a weight of responsibility with good grace was little short of bizarre. The bridegroom seemed genuinely protective of his family and concerned that Isabel and Marcus should not have wanted during his absence. He acted like a man doing more than his duty.

Suddenly Edgar felt his chest swelling in satisfaction and pride. Like the rest of the *ton,* Edgar knew this man kept a lady of rare beauty as his mistress. Yet for two pins he would wager his new son-in-law was enamoured of his Isabel. He couldn't have selected a finer husband for her from amongst the best Almack's had to offer at a Wednesday assembly. He might be somewhat tardy, but Isabel's prodigal beau had returned to claim her...as she had always said he would.

Edgar mumbled deep in his throat, 'I suppose there's no point in being at loggerheads. I expect I might have done things better for Isabel and the child. He seems a nice little chap...and fair and handsome with it. The boy favours our side.'

'Marcus.'

'Eh?'

'My son's name is Marcus.'

'Yes...Marcus. That's it. You're a lucky man to get a son. I've daughters and three of the four have put me through the mill, I can tell you. Even the youngest, Sylvie, is promising to top the lot for wilful insubordination.' He took a fortifying gulp of wine. 'We have just returned from visiting her at her finishing school. We were summoned by the Principal.' He shook his sparsely covered head and moaned. 'Sylvie has it in her head to quit her education and become a missionary in Africa! Before that Rachel was no end of trouble to me until Connor, bless him, took her off my hands. Thank heavens June was biddable and sweet. She would be welcomed back home at any time, but she has been married for two years to a good chap and no problems there.'

Etienne dwelled on William Pemberton's overnight stay at White's. In his humble opinion all might not be right there but, with the reticence of a man who knows it wise to get his own house in order before he comments on others, he kept quiet. His sympathy for his father-in-law's ordeals in rearing girls was thus limited to a neutral grunt.

His mind lingered with great tenderness on one of those wayward daughters. His brave noble wife had fought like a tigress to safeguard his baby. She had shunned her family's advice and refused to give up Marcus or revile her seducer for abandoning her. With sweet trust and innocence she'd believed he also cherished the memory of their loving. Etienne felt the breathtaking tightening in his chest and, for the first time since he was a boy watching his parents' bitter fights, felt he might weep with the inalterable anguish of it all.

'Anyway, I'm not that much of a wealthy man.'

From a long way off Etienne heard the sly grumble and focused on it. It helped him force a quirk of a smile. 'You must let me know what I owe you for providing for my wife and son in my absence.'

Edgar waved a dismissing hand. 'No... no...wouldn't dream of it...' he muttered beneath his breath.

'But I insist.'

'I'll send over the account.' Edgar picked up his glass and drained it.

The following day at the appointed hour June and William Pemberton came to visit. While the gentlemen repaired to Etienne's study to talk and supervise from a window three young scamps scaling the apple trees, the ladies opted to take a drive for it was a mild day in early spring.

'It is so good to see you, Isabel. I can't believe that this day is finally come.' With a burst of sisterly affection, June leaned forward and spontaneously embraced her sister before resettling on the seat of her smart barouche. 'I would have written more often. And visited more often but for Papa being so very worried that regular contact might lead to the secret being uncovered and set malicious tongues wagging. Now I think he and Mama are more concerned that Sylvie will blight her own chance of marriage. She has some rather odd ideas, I must say. She insists she will travel the globe before settling down. It is not a good idea: she is far too pretty to safely undertake such shenanigans.'

Isabel smiled. 'Papa told Etienne that Sylvie is keen to become a missionary in Africa.'

June's face was a picture of appalled distaste. 'Heavens!' was all she said.

'Etienne met William in White's. He says that William is a very happy man.'

'Is he, indeed? I wish he would tell that to me once in a while,' June declared roundly.

Isabel frowned. Despite being away from June for years, they had slipped easily into sisterly intimacy. 'You are very happy too, June, aren't you?'

June looked a little ill at ease. She sighed, 'Yes, of course; most of the time. It's nothing.' A languid hand was used to dispel Isabel's concerned frown. 'We had a little tiff because of his mother. She knows exactly how to stir things up between us. I don't know why I let the old besom bother me.' June shrugged and sighed. 'Have you met Etienne's relations?'

'Only his mother: Claudine seems pleasant enough. She is French. His father is dead and he has a sister, Monique, who is married with twin children. Oh, and he has grandparents in Cambridge on whom he seems to dote, although he would have one believe otherwise.'

June's sweet face animated archly. 'You two get on well together, don't you? It's amazing he found you so far from York and not knowing you were connected in any way to Connor.'

The smile that sprang unbidden to Isabel's lips was exceedingly wry. 'It is good Marcus has his father at last but…things have not been easy between us. I can't pretend that Etienne was overjoyed to discover he had a son and responsibilities. He was virtually spoken for elsewhere, you know.'

Isabel shrugged. '*Virtually* is nothing. Half the *ton* is on the point of becoming betrothed, if one believes the tattle. Anyway, Caroline Greenwood has been making sheep's eyes at Lord Fairbright for ages. He must have been…surprised…'

'Who…Lord Fairbright?'

'No! Etienne must have been surprised to discover he was a father.'

'I think flabbergasted is a better description.'

'Well, for all that, you seem so…right together.' June took her sister's hand and squeezed it encouragingly. 'I imagine no couple has a perfect marriage. But sometimes I suppose it might be wise to turn a blind eye to men's weaknesses and peccadilloes.'

Isabel smiled at the passing street scene. 'I take it from that piece of advice that you are aware Etienne is in love with Lady Avery.'

'I know she is his mistress. Was his mistress,' June quickly corrected. 'I'm sure it is all in the past, Isabel. You seem to deal so…so naturally together. And his eyes are on you all the time with a certain look.'

'He's probably checking I don't disgrace him in company.' Feeling ashamed of the petulant remark and knowing it to be untrue, Isabel sighed. 'It is having Marcus between us that has made us endeavour to be compatible. There is much to arrange for our son's future.' Isabel paused before reflecting sadly, 'It will never be a marriage as happy as yours. Etienne does love Lady Avery. He honestly told me straight away that he would always be close to her even after he married. But it doesn't matter. He has done his duty and been good to us.'

Chapter Fifteen

'You look beautiful.'

'Thank you.'

Felicity Wright suppressed a pleased little smile on overhearing the master's compliment and her mistress's shy response. The erstwhile man of her dreams had greeted her by name and barely given her a glance on passing moments earlier. Undismayed, the maid tactfully withdrew into the dressing room through which Colonel Hauke had recently gained entry to his wife's sleeping quarters.

Peeking out at them, while gathering up combs and brushes from the dressing stand, Felicity's female eye appreciated a lofty masculine frame in profile. Charcoal tailcoat and breeches, a starched white cuff, a stylish shoe that looked like Reeves had sweated over shining it... Indeed, he was a looker, she chuckled to herself. And her mistress *was* a beauty. She wondered now how she'd ever thought her plain. Mrs Hauke's hair might not be flaxen, but it slipped like silk skeins across her hand when she brushed it. And no tongs needed to curl it! Her complexion wasn't roses, but it was fine and unblemished and needed no powder or patch. *And* she was a lady with a good heart. Felicity more than any knew that. She slanted another squint at the handsome couple. In Felicity's estimation a woman who wore grey and whose hair looked like a nag's mane just couldn't compete with *her* heroine, no matter how refined she might be. Silver cushions! She scoffed as she quietly closed the door and went about her business.

Eyes as glossy as summer grass briefly merged with an earthy gaze reflected in the mirror. Isabel fiddled with the neat pearls at her throat with nervous fingers. More than a month married and this was the first time her husband had invaded her unlocked citadel. A tight curl was coaxed to unravel on to a fragile collarbone. Her plucking was unnecessary; Felicity had made a competent job of styling her hair. 'Are you waiting for me? Am I late?' It was an abrupt query, aimed to stir him from simply studying her with low-lidded eyes concealing his expression.

'No, we've plenty of time…'

Isabel jumped up from her stool in front of the dressing table. 'I'm not sure I can go through with this folly.' She spun away from him in a rustle of leafy silk, ashamed of her cowardice.

'Yes, you can. I'll be close at all times if you need me.' His voice was honey sweet and suddenly he was behind her. His breath stirred her hair and muscular arms drew her back inexorably against him. Warm lips grazed her nape, making her shiver, then instinctively melt against his hard body. Gladly she accepted his comfort…before she stiffened. Intruding into her languor was one of the reasons she wanted to cry off their first social engagement as man and wife. The thought of being brought face to face with Lady Avery was daunting.

Sensing her frigidity, Etienne moved away. 'I have brought you something to wear.' He withdrew an elegant rectangular case from his pocket and snapped it open. 'It occurs to me I've been tardy in presenting you with a wedding gift.'

Isabel blinked at the dazzling flower bursts of emeralds and diamonds planted in platinum. Never before had she seen such an exquisite suite of jewellery. Her stony eyes tore away from the awesome sight. 'You gave me a wedding ring. That was all I ever wanted,' she rebuffed proudly as unsteady fingers rotated the plain band.

'I know that's all you wanted,' he soothed. 'But I contest meanness joining other crimes you may hold against me. You're my bride and I should like you to accept my wedding gift.'

Her eyes stole back to glorious gems. Her Aunt Florence's pearls were the only jewellery of worth she possessed. Take it! a stubborn inner voice scolded her diffidence. Why should you not enjoy his bounty? A smart carriage and matching horses cost a pretty penny. If he sees fit to lavish gifts on his mistress, why should his wife not enjoy a little luxury too?

'I thank you for your generosity. I have no wedding gift for you, I'm afraid.'

'Nothing at all to bestow?' he asked with ironical inflection and a glint of sultry humour in his eyes. 'Are you sure?' After a tense pause he added wryly, 'There's no need to look quite so alarmed, Isabel. I'd settle for a kiss.'

Isabel felt the sting of blood warm her cheeks, but returned composedly, 'I believe I might have something to give you actually. It's of little monetary value. Nevertheless, I'm sure Marcus would like you to have it until he is old enough to make use of it himself.' She had swept to the chest of drawers in the corner whilst speaking and withdrew a small battered casket.

In solemn silence gifts were exchanged.

Isabel looked on anxiously as he opened the ring box. 'It belonged to my grandfather: my papa's father. When Marcus had his first birthday my papa sent it to him as a gift. I know it is rather worn…' She noticed then the solid square signet ring that already adorned a long patrician finger and wished she had kept her precious paltry heirloom to herself. The disparity in their gifts seemed ridiculous. 'Its charm lies in its sentimental value. I wouldn't expect you to wear it. It's just a token.'

Etienne removed the ring from its thread-bare bed. He smiled as the pitted gold slid snugly over an olive knuckle. 'Perfect fit,' he said and held up his left hand for her to inspect his wedding ring.

'How odd,' she remarked on a little laugh. 'He was not at all your size. He was quite short and tubby. He was my favourite grandparent— a lovely kind gentleman.'

'Then I'll always wear it. Perhaps it will transfer some virtue to me.' Etienne pulled her slowly towards him and his lips brushed on hers. 'Thank you.'

Taking the jewellery case from her hand, he placed it down then turned her gently about. He removed the delicate warm pearls and re-placed them with weighty gems that stroked with icy sensuousness against her throat. Her fingers went up immediately to touch the hard lustrous stones as he urged her to inspect her reflection in the pier glass.

'Do you like it?'

'It's beautiful.' She glanced down at the other pieces in the parure: eardrops and a dainty tiara, a bracelet, and the *pièce de résistance,* a cabochon emerald and diamond ring. 'It's all so very beautiful.'

'I'm pleased it finds favour. I hoped you would like emeralds. I wasn't sure what to choose. But as they match your eyes and you like to wear green...'

'Yes, I do. It's one of the few colours that suits me.'

Etienne raised a hand, skimmed his dark knuckles along the side of a pale satiny jaw. 'Anything would suit you, you're almost perfect.'

'Almost? A comment like that is certain to raise female hackles...and curiosity. In which way must I improve?' It was lightly said; in fact she felt gayer than she had all day.

'Be more demonstrative in your gratitude.'

Isabel felt herself submerging in his rakish charm, in the lambent amber lights bathing her. She tore her eyes away from his. 'Don't!'

'Don't what?'

'Don't treat me like a fool. Don't flirt. Don't pretend that this marriage is anything more than a sham,' was fired at him in a rapid burst. 'If you now want us to be friends...good! I am glad! There is no need for you to—'

'For me to—?'

'All this…this wooing,' exploded from her tightly, her frustration manifesting in a whirling hand. 'Don't do it. Please! It is all so…so unnecessary, in any case. We both know it is false. If you must flirt, do so with your good friend. Save all your seduction for Lady Avery.'

For a moment he simply looked at her while a silence roared between them. A withering laugh grazed his throat, a barely audible oath followed. Within a moment he was by the door. 'In case you are interested, Isabel, since we were married the only good friend I have had is you.' With that he left her alone.

'You didn't really imagine I'd let you face all the malicious battleaxes on your own, did you? After I received Mama's note bringing me up to date, and I realised you were not in Suffolk but still in London, I knew the old tabbies would have their claws out for you. I would have swum the Irish Sea if necessary to get here in time. Thankfully Connor's yacht cracks along at quite a speed.'

Isabel smiled. 'I'm so glad you are here, Rachel. Although I did have dear June for moral support, you know.' She squeezed at her younger sister's arm.

Rachel chuckled. 'The more Merediths present the better. It is a shame Sylvie is not also here. It would be that imp's idea of a great prank to arrive at Lord Fairbright's ball before she has attained her sixteenth birthday or made her come out. That infamy would really make them snort at their salts.'

Isabel's eyes skipped nervously over groups of people. Some guests seemed unabashed to openly glare their disgust; others were secreting their despising behind quivering fans or sly eyelids. Quite a few gentlemen appeared to be using unemployed drinking vessels as shields over which to ogle them.

Rachel announced cheerfully, 'I imagine we shall be under siege on all sides. The petticoat brigade must be grinding away tooth enamel now that Colonel Hauke is no longer available, and the old besoms are bound to be eager to rummage in our cupboard now the skeleton has evacuated.'

'We should use military tactics,' June chipped in. 'If we become separated and surrounded, we must divulge only name and rank, then retreat and regroup, by this pillar, to launch a counter-attack.'

A mutual giggle mingled as the three young women came close together in an affectionate embrace that proclaimed loyalty and solidarity to their audience.

'What *would* I do without you two?' Isabel murmured with a catch to her voice. She knew her two dear sisters were doing their utmost to boost her courage with their support. She was exceedingly grateful. Yet people were entitled to deplore her outrageous past, even that heroic version her husband had concocted. She didn't allow her mind to dwell on the *ton*'s private reaction should it ever discover the base truth.

Here and there about the vast ballroom were stationed groups of young débutantes, eyeing her with sulky disdain. They would not deviate from fastidious observation of rules and etiquette before marriage. To them her wantonness must fly beyond the pale.

From the corner of an eye Isabel could just glimpse the man who had made her again ac-

ceptable, if not welcome. His physical presence wasn't strictly necessary. Now she could
mingle in society with her sisters or her parents
and not risk a demand she be ejected from decent company. She was a married woman, protected by her husband's name. And she was
envied. Bright bitter eyes that raked her person
made that clear.

Isabel sniffed and tipped her head to a
haughty angle. Humiliation could wait for another day. 'Let battle commence,' she announced with a defiant glint animating eyes
that rivalled the lustrous emeralds she wore.
Linking arms with her allies, she urged them
in perfect time and satin slippers to gracefully
march towards the ballroom.

Behind the trio of blond beauties, close
enough to be escorts, yet at a distance that respected their independence, strolled three urbane men.

Connor slanted a look at his friend's tense
jaw. 'Relax,' he advised. 'Rachel won't let
anyone succeed in insulting her.'

'Neither will I,' Etienne responded quietly
without removing his eyes from the subject of
his vigilance.

'Women can be vicious cats,' William Pemberton remarked as his gaze skipped about and found the reason he was well acquainted with that particular aspect of the female character. His mother, resplendent in violet satin, acknowledged his attention with a gracious smile.

Receiving a minimal response, Pamela Pemberton's eyes shifted from her son to her daughter-in-law. She still found it hard to understand why her dear boy had chosen to marry beneath him, and to such a mouse. Her eyes narrowed as they encompassed the two other Meredith girls. Hardly timid, they! Rachel had always been an incorrigible little madam and now the world knew that Isabel had long been an incorrigible little minx. Both had, nevertheless, netted husbands that would make a duke's daughter bilious with envy. In fact, Pamela was hard pressed to know if she felt more in awe than in judgement of Isabel's infamous conduct. She was certainly casting a covetous eye over the magnificent gems the hussy had about her person. Naturally she was scandalised, as were most people, to discover that Isabel Meredith had not been lost years

ago to disease but to disgrace. But what a res-
urrection! She was back in circulation with a
distinguished husband close by her side. The
Colonel had been one of the most sought-after
bachelors during the previous season. Little
wonder the Merediths had the gall to look so
preposterously pleased with themselves.

Edgar squeezed his wife's hand. 'Chin up,
my dear, and smile. It is our Bella's big day.
We might have missed her nuptials, but we are
here to witness her reception back into society.'

'Can she emerge from the embers without
getting a serious scald?' Gloria whispered via
a smile that was making her jaw ache.

'Indeed she can!' Edgar hissed back encouragingly. 'And what feathers has our phoe-
nix! Look at those sparklers. My goodness, he
has done her proud. She couldn't want for anything more.'

Gloria managed to quell his jubilance with
a severe stare. From a corner of her mouth
emerged, 'Isabel has need of affection, too,
you know. Does he *love* her, do you think?'

Edgar's chuckle transformed to a grimace as
words spat through his teeth. 'You think a man
spends that sort of cash on someone he *likes?*'

Gloria looked a mite mollified.

'I fear it is not a mutual regard, Gloria,' Edgar sighed out below his breath. 'She seems a little…reserved with him. She ought to be overjoyed he has made her respectable.'

'I'm sure she loves him still,' Gloria muttered.

'She ought soon make it plain, if she does. He has another attachment, you know. A man in demand don't wear his heart on his sleeve for long.'

'She'll let him know when the time is right, Edgar.' Slipping her hand through her husband's arm Gloria urged him forward. 'Come…let us greet our beautiful girls.'

'Well! The brass-faced cheek of it!'

Pamela Pemberton felt her companion's fingers nip her arm then shake it in emphasis.

'Look! The shameless little trollop is actually parading like she hasn't a care in the world. I'm surprised she didn't bring along her bastard to flaunt. I've heard tell the boy's blond and nothing like the Colonel!'

'Hush, Mama! Someone will hear you.' Caroline Greenwood was grouped with her mother and her mother's friend. She frowned her disapproval, then took a quick, circumspect look this way and that.

'I hope they all *do* hear. I'm not afraid to declare I'm disgusted. I'm only saying what others think.' Noting a few sympathetic eyes on her, she responded with a satisfied twitch of the lips. 'In my opinion the Colonel's been tricked by those crafty Merediths. If the baggage ever *was* a camp follower, I dare say she couldn't identify which redcoat sired the wretch. In my opinion there is a less glamorous explanation for such a scandal than seduction and shipwrecks.'

'He must idolise her to have given her such wonderful jewellery,' Caroline said stubbornly.

'It makes one wonder what she did to get them.' Insinuation coarsened Pamela Pemberton's voice and lifted one thin eyebrow.

'I imagine it was the same thing as got her the brat,' Mrs Greenwood sneered.

Caroline blanched, then blushed. Her large eyes swivelled about to detect eavesdroppers. *'Mama!'* she protested. 'Please don't make your…your *disappointment* so vulgar. I truly don't mind that Colonel Hauke has married someone else. He never actually proposed to me.'

'I doubt he ever actually *proposed* to *her* either. But she's got him down the aisle. And so could you have done with a little more effort. One day you would have been a countess. Now we are a laughing stock.'

'We would not have been, Mama, had you not started wedding preparations prematurely.'

Pamela Pemberton was quite entertained by the unhappy dialogue between mother and daughter. The tale circulating about the Colonel and his lady *did* beggar belief. It was because of that most people accepted it as true. Etienne Hauke had forgone an alliance with the Greenwoods, which would have earned him a small fortune, to make an honest woman of the mother of his son.

Along with her cronies, with whom she had savoured the tale's juicy details long into the previous night, Pamela had felt a delightful frisson over the romantic and raffish appeal of it all. All the ladies in her coterie had been impatient to scrutinise Isabel's appearance to see whether in their opinions she was a beauty worthy to star in such a drama. Pamela had to admit that, whilst not as strikingly lovely as Rachel, the heroine was decidedly pretty in a rather winsome way.

'Colonel Hauke has spread the news about their relationship. I don't see why he would lie about any of it, Mama.' Caroline challenged her boiling-countenanced mother.

'I don't see why he would lie either,' Pamela concurred, simply to stir the pot.

'And neither do I,' said a dulcet, cultured voice at their shoulders. 'In fact, I own that I know it all to be true.'

Pamela gave Lady Valerie Avery a nervous smile whilst wondering how on earth they had merited such a notable's attention. Lady Avery moved in quite exalted circles and, but for an acknowledgement now and again, ignored her little clique. 'We were just saying, Lady Avery, we recognise the ring of truth to it all. Why would the Colonel fabricate a story?'

'Why indeed? He is one of the most honest men I know.'

'Of course, you *know* him well, Lady Avery,' Mrs Greenwood fawned venomously.

'That is also true.' Valerie Avery allowed a smile. 'I've known him very well indeed for a long time. We were good friends at the time of the…incident, and I can thus vouch for its veracity. I can remember quite clearly how distraught the Colonel was when he returned from overseas having been a prisoner of war.'

'You *knew* that Colonel Hauke thought he had lost his beloved in tragic circumstances? He *told* you that?' Mrs Greenwood lost subtlety as her inquisitiveness escalated.

'I was his confidante. We discussed everything: happy and sad. More than that I cannot say for fear of betraying trust…you understand.'

With twin expressions of sage sympathy both Mrs Greenwood and Mrs Pemberton nodded at Lady Avery.

Caroline stirred herself from her embarrassed daze. It was an open secret that Lady Avery was the Colonel's mistress and had kept that coveted place in his life for many years.

At one time, when her mother was fretting the Colonel wasn't keen enough in his courtship, she had directed her to copy this woman's look and style. But though her hair was dark, it had a stubborn curl to it and resisted being sleek. Her skin with its tendency to high colour would not whiten no matter what amount of powder her mother pressed on to it. Caroline had been mortified when she ended up looking like a marionette with scraped-down hair and red spots of colour breaking through her *maquillage.*

Lady Avery smiled at Caroline with an amount of encouraging empathy. It helped Caroline find her voice. 'I think the Colonel must be very proud of his wife. In my opinion, Isabel Meredith has been extremely brave.'

'I think so too,' Lady Avery agreed. 'In fact, I desire to tell her so. Do you?' Valerie's eyes held a glint of challenge.

Caroline took a glance at her mother's dropping jaw. *Her* chin went up. 'I do, Lady Avery. Yes…I *do.*'

Chapter Sixteen

'Three of the finest catches the *ton* has ever had on offer are *our* sons-in-law.'

'I know, my dear,' Edgar said. 'And I think that fact irks some of these females more than the beauty of our daughters.' He turned about with the intention of casting a contented eye on those distinguished gentlemen. His desultory gaze snagged on a sight that made him groan then splutter. 'Oh, my heavens! Look who is almost upon us, Gloria!'

'Mr and Mrs Meredith! How nice it is to see you again. It has been some while, has it not? I think we last met at Rosemary Clairborne's *musicale*.' Valerie Avery graciously inclined her head at Gloria's jerky bob and Edgar's equally ungainly bow. 'I am acquainted with June, of course. Will you not introduce me to your other two daughters?'

Edgar manfully expanded a pigeon-chest, opened his mouth to utterly defend his brood. Alas, no sound issued. He turned an appealing look on his wife.

'Indeed…of course, Lady Avery, let me introduce you to Rachel…Isabel, too,' Gloria weakly babbled.

At the mention of Lady Avery's name, Isabel had frozen, ceased hearing Rachel talk to her friend, Lucinda, and pivoted about.

Calm grey eyes featured first in Isabel's observation. Then she saw sleek jet hair. The woman's other attributes merged into a painful awareness of exquisite beauty and a pearl-grey gown shimmering over a shapely figure. Quite remotely she realised she would have recognised her from her servants' description. Refinement seemed to bathe the atmosphere in which she beatifically breathed. It was little consolation to know she was possibly Etienne's age, if not a year or two older.

'Lady Avery, this is my daughter Isabel. *Mrs* Isabel *Hauke*,' Gloria robustly emphasised as maternal instinct asserted itself.

The immediate vicinity was quietening as conversations withered and people strained to

overhear what was being said. The unantici-
pated meeting between the wife, the mistress
and the fiancée was a fascinating and welcome
spectacle.

If Lady Avery was aware her civility had
engendered such gawping, she chose to ignore
it. With true aplomb she extended a hand of
welcome to Isabel.

Where are you, Etienne? Why are you not
equally suffering this excruciating situation?
The pressing thought was drumming an ache
in Isabel's head. It had not occurred to her that
her husband's mistress would boldly solicit an
introduction to her lover's wife the moment the
reprobate disappeared.

Yet there was no malice in Lady Avery's
mild demeanour. In fact, a gentle pleading
seemed to radiate from her eyes as though begging her pardon, begging her understanding.
Slowly Isabel extended her emerald-weighted
fingers.

Valerie Avery gratefully received those fingers, squeezed them in welcome. With Isabel's
hand still in hers, she drew forward Caroline
who she then introduced.

'We felt we must come and tell you we are pleased to meet you. And also convey our felicitations on your marriage, Mrs Hauke.' Valerie's speech was accompanied by a reassuring smile for every vigilant Meredith. Rachel had now stopped chatting to her friends and had joined her parents and June, protectively close to Isabel. 'You have been away from London for a long while. It is not always an easy environment to return to. You have braved it and we admire your courage.' Valerie continued undisturbed by the hushed auditorium. 'We sincerely welcome you back and wish you much happiness.'

'I…yes…thank you,' Isabel said and looked quickly at Rachel, who was listening intently as though prepared to intervene at the first hint of offence.

'My eldest daughter, Rachel Flinte, Countess of Devane.' Gloria realised she had been remiss in that introduction.

Valerie Avery extended a hand to Rachel, too. 'You are to be congratulated, Mrs Meredith. Three beautiful blond daughters and another I believe at home. How very lucky you are.'

'We were only just saying the very same thing,' Edgar burst out, all *bonhomie* now his guard had been lowered by the lady's disarming charm. 'Sylvie is at school and already as handsome as her sisters.'

'Blond hair is divine. I hear your son is blond, Mrs Hauke.' Caroline had sincerely intended to be amenable. But her complexion became ruddy on recalling her mother's spiteful remark that the boy was nothing like his swarthy father. 'I expect he is like you.'

'He is a little like me,' Isabel kindly agreed.

'Perhaps in the future we might take a drive in the park together, Mrs Hauke. My nephew Robert is eight and likes the menagerie. Perhaps we could go there with your son... or...or somewhere else?'

Isabel understood, in such a unique situation as they found themselves, it was difficult to weigh the constraints of etiquette with a desire to be friendly. Caroline was endeavouring to capture just that balance and Isabel's heart went out to her. Suddenly she felt an inner spring of tension uncoil. This was not some malicious ploy by two females with ulterior motives. With simple insight she realised her husband's mistress and his rejected fiancée had, against all odds, chosen to join her as allies. She smiled with shy, sweet gratitude. 'I would be delighted...Marcus would be delighted...to go with you to the zoo.'

'We must not take up all your time,' Valerie said. 'I see there are other people waiting to speak to you.'

Isabel's eyes darted about. Incredibly there were now quite a few people jostling for position, trying to catch her eye with a smile, as though keen for an introduction.

As they walked away, Valerie patted at Caroline's hand, revealing her relief that a tricky situation had been successfully overcome. 'I see Lord Fairbright is looking a little bereft now the ladies are all keen to be introduced to Mrs Hauke and her entourage. I expect our host might like an attractive young lady to talk to.' Her dismissal was mitigated by a smile. She walked on gracefully alone.

'So tell me...how many times were you a prisoner of war?'

Etienne spun on a heel and squinted into the darkness. A white grin split his dark face as he recognised the identity of the man silhouetted in the gloom. Leaving Connor and William leaning on the terrace railing, smoking, he strolled over. 'As many times as I need to be.'

The fellow laughed, flicking away the smouldering stub of a cigar into the night. 'I've always loved a romantic tale...and a misbehaved woman.'

'Yes, I remember.' Etienne said wryly. 'I was just thinking the other day that I hoped I'd run into you. Have you still got that temperamental white stallion? I forget his name.'

'White stallion?'

'I borrowed him to take to York...eight years ago.'

'Ah! I remember; *that* temperamental white stallion. Star. He's out to graze at Stratton Manor.'

'I'll buy him from you.'

'I'll have him sent over. No charge. Wedding present.'

Etienne gave a nod in appreciation of the man's generosity. 'How is Elizabeth?'

'She's very well. She was talking to your wife a little while ago. She wanted to approach her immediately you arrived, but I advised her to wait. Then, just as Elizabeth was about to make her move, Lady Avery and Miss Greenwood beat her to it. Thereafter a queue formed.'

Etienne's dark eyes narrowed on his companion. A curse hissed out through his teeth.

'It wasn't a problem. It was a very astute move, actually. I have to say I admire your taste in women...all of them. The righteous are now falling over themselves to be nice to your wife.'

Etienne peered over a shoulder at the French doors and then set out towards them at quite a pace. He turned, walked backwards as he called to his erstwhile army comrade, 'Thanks for the wedding present, Trelawney. You and Elizabeth must visit us...'

'Don't run away...please.'

When he was a step away from a globe of golden light spilling from the ballroom, that throaty plea lured Etienne back into the shadow of a mulberry tree.

'Don't be angry with me. I can see from your face that you are.'

'I'm not angry, Valerie. I hear I should be thanking you.'

Valerie Avery's mouth twisted ruefully. 'But you won't. You're more concerned with knowing whether I have upset your wife. I haven't, Etienne, I promise.' A careless touch on his arm contrasted with vivid melancholy in her eyes. 'I too must say thank you. Thank you for letting me show the world that it is I who bring our friendship to a dignified close. And I have done so at the first opportunity. You wanted to allow me that one small scrap of comfort…didn't you? That is why I have seen nothing of you, heard nothing from you, isn't it, Etienne?'

Etienne gave a small wry smile. 'Yes.' In truth, he had hoped that his mistress would allow her pride to dictate her future. He would have hated it to be obvious that he was putting off a woman who pined for him. Valerie had shown him nothing but loyalty and devotion for many years; the last thing he wanted was her humiliation. 'You're far too young for a pension, Valerie,' he said softly. 'I knew you wouldn't want that.'

'No. I wanted you to marry Miss Greenwood. Then nothing would have changed between us,' she said with a raw throb to her voice.

Etienne bowed his head, examined the toes of his shoes. 'I'm sorry…very sorry…'

'Don't be! We all deserve to fall in love. If one is lucky enough to fall in love with one's spouse, how wonderful that must be. I understand. She seems sweet…'

Etienne missed the hint of cattishness as he choked on a laugh. *'Sweet?'* He tested the epithet. The single word bonded longing and exasperation and an affection that made Valerie's last hope that he might succumb to seduction shrivel and die.

'I see you are restless to be off. Just one last thing, Etienne…' She quickly went on to tiptoe and pressed her soft lips hard against his, as though she would weld them together forever by that touching patch of skin. His response was minimal, no more than polite. Valerie forced a light laugh. 'That was just a little parting gift…for old times' sake. Almost eleven years and yet I can recall as though it were yesterday the time we met.'

It was the impatient glance over her shoulder that helped her to step away. 'I wish you happiness, my love.' In a moment she had disappeared into the throng in the ballroom in a rustle of silver satin.

Etienne closed his eyes and a curse sighed beneath his breath. Having acknowledged he was a bastard, he turned towards the French doors with relief swamping him that the deed was done. He glimpsed a flash of green on the periphery of his vision but was so intent on finding Isabel he unwisely gave it little thought.

In the weeks that followed Isabel found she could have socialised every evening had she so desired. Invitations to balls, soirées, and all manner of functions arrived daily. Some were addressed to her and Etienne as a couple; others were for her as lady of the house. On the rare occasions in the evening that her husband appeared to dine, Isabel civilly consulted him as to which they might attend.

Neither of them had ever mentioned that first outing as newlyweds when Lady Avery had set the seal on her approval by polite society. Isabel had kept to herself the anguish she had felt on witnessing such a tender scene between Etienne and his mistress. She knew he had immediately sensed her coolness after he joined her in Lord Fairbright's ballroom. Soon after they had left and returned home in frosty silence. The awful irony was that she had been happily searching for him on the terrace to tell him that she was beginning to relax and enjoy herself when she caught him kissing Lady Avery.

When making a fleet-footed retreat that night, the motive for Lady Avery's largesse had become woundingly apparent. It had been a finely timed charade. Etienne had no doubt persuaded his mistress to patronise his wife and her family whilst he loitered outside. And Lady Avery had done so, to great effect, and had been rewarded with a kiss. The lovers had obviously believed the gauche wife to be out of sight. But then perhaps they believed they were too, tucked beneath the spreading branches of the mulberry tree. It was simply a shimmer of silver as the moon fled a cloud that had betrayed them.

Isabel's faraway gaze focused on her coffee cup. She picked it up and sipped, grimacing as the lukewarm liquid filmed her lips. She pushed the beverage away and with it her uneaten toast.

She stared out over an expanse of polished wood to the place it would be usual to see one's spouse in the morning at breakfast. But of course he was not there. He was rarely there and when she did see him she had too much pride to demand to know where he spent his nights, or with whom.

Besides, she knew the answer to that. She had no need or inclination to embarrass either of them by becoming emotional or clingy. And what right had she to condemn him? She had told him to use his flirtatious seduction on Lady Avery. He had no need to know that she frequently wished she could retract such stupid words and conquer her pride enough to say she loved him, that she had never stopped loving him, and could they please try to be happy. Instead, they came together from time to time and conversed in the language of spare formal politeness as if they were strangers.

She thought of her plans for the day. Caroline Greenwood would arrive later. They were going to Madame Tussaud's Waxworks with Robert Wilson, Caroline's nephew, and

Marcus. The boys had played together before and had got along famously.

Caroline had been sipping tea with Isabel in the sitting room after their expedition to the menagerie when Etienne had unexpectedly arrived home. Considering that once they had been on the point of becoming betrothed, neither Etienne nor Caroline seemed particularly uneasy in the other's presence. As Caroline had reassuringly told Isabel on their first outing to Hyde Park, it had been an arrangement of convenience, not courtship.

The banging front door brought Isabel to her senses. Automatically she reached for her cup and took a fortifying gulp of unpleasantly scummy coffee. She was replacing the cup with a grimace on her face when her husband entered the dining room.

Dark eyes slanted at her from a gaunt, unshaven face. 'Is that scowl anything to do with my arrival?'

The sardonic tone he used made her colour heighten. 'No. The coffee is cold.' She noted he was pouring himself a cup from the silver pot on the sideboard. 'Shall I get some fresh brought in for you?'

Etienne took a cautious sip. 'This is fine.'

'The pot must have kept it hot. Mine was cold in the cup.' Isabel fell silent. Why on earth was she justifying her expression of distaste for cold coffee? 'Would you like something to eat?'

'No. I'll breakfast with Connor. I'm only home to clean up.' Another look arrowed her way as though he expected her spirits might lighten at that comment. 'We have some business to attend to.'

'More business?' Isabel shrilled gaily. 'How very enterprising of you! Every day you have so many deals to keep you busy…and abroad. Meetings with Connor and William and Mr Greenwood…'

'It's how I afford to keep us all in the style to which we've become accustomed.'

Isabel flushed and her eyes flinched from his, prompting an oath beneath his breath and a hand to swipe the bluish bristle on his face. 'I'm sorry, Isabel. That was a stupid, churlish thing to say. All I meant was that I have a few unforeseen expenses, and money that isn't readily accessible to meet them at present.

Besides, I thought my absence would please you.'

'You don't need to explain to me,' Isabel rebuffed as she gained her feet. 'A wife and a child foisted on to one must be financially burdensome, I'm sure.'

'It's not you or Marcus that's a problem. Do you want me to be home more?'

'Not if you would rather be somewhere else.'

'What is that supposed to mean?' he demanded. On seeing her whitening face, he banged down his cup. 'God's teeth! Why do we always end in arguing?'

'Possibly it is because we spend so little time together that misunderstandings arise.'

'I need to stay away, Isabel. I need to keep busy. It helps stop me being...'

'Being *what?* Being at home?'

'Being frustrated,' he gritted through barely moving teeth.

'I'm sorry I have ruined your life and your prospects.'

A look at her indignant face had him choking a laugh. 'It is *not* that sort of frustrated,

Isabel. You've not thwarted any ambition I had that was worth a moment's pause.'

She looked curiously at him before blushing.

'Yes, *that* frustrated,' he muttered with a mix of amusement and apology. 'Where is Marcus?' he asked, turning away.

'His tutor is with him. Later we are going to see the waxworks. It is a shame you never accompany us on such trips.'

'I know. I would today but I have promised your brothers-in-law to meet them at the Palm House. We have documents to sign.'

'Yes. I understand.'

'I don't think you do, Isabel. I don't think you want to understand what's wrong in this marriage. But you're not so naïve. We made a baby after all, didn't we?'

Isabel flinched, expecting the door to slam as he went out, but it closed quietly and she stood motionless, crying, listening to his footsteps die away.

Both Rachel and June joined Isabel and Caroline on the outing to the waxworks. Later the boys wanted to sail boats in Hyde Park's lake before returning home.

June linked arms with Isabel and sighed as they paraded the perimeter of the park. 'It is a shame our poor husbands are stuck in a dingy office with a dusty old lawyer instead of taking the air with us.'

Isabel smiled neutrally.

'Of course, they will enjoy this afternoon's entertainment.'

'Will they?' Isabel enquired lightly.

'Did Etienne not say? There is a boxing bout arranged between an English and a French fighter at Gentleman Jackson's.'

'Oh.'

Marcus rushed up to his mother and thrust a dripping wooden yacht into her hands. 'May Robert come back with us for tea?'

'Of course,' his mother told him.

At five of the clock Connor and William arrived to join them for tea and to take their respective wives home.

'Is Etienne not with you?' Rachel asked Connor conversationally about their host's absence.

Isabel barely faltered in encouraging Robert to have more cake.

'I haven't seen Etienne since we left Bank Street. He didn't watch the match. He received a note and went off in a hurry...'

Conversation died, the room quietened, and Isabel knew without looking up to see expressions that embarrassment had settled on the company. Most men, she realised with a quiver of despair, would be grateful for such devoted attention from Valerie Avery.

With a smile fixed on her face, Isabel stood up with the cake plate and insisted everyone must have more.

Chapter Seventeen

It was in the unendurably long hour between darkness and dawn that Isabel decided things must change.

Once the die was cast she was unable to sleep further and climbed from her warm bed. A moon scudded out from beneath a quilt of cloud to stripe mercurial light through the wide chink in the curtains. She lit tapers quickly, then took a few moments dislodging her travelling trunk from the top of the clothes press. By candlelight she calmly started opening drawers in the chests and packing her clothes.

An irrepressible urge drew her eyes to the dressing-room door. She let the chemise in her hand drop into the case and glided trance-like through no-man's land. Without hesitating for a moment she turned a handle and trespassed for the first time.

She approached her husband's bed on noiseless feet, mounted the small dais on which the four-poster grandly reposed, and gazed forlornly down at undisturbed pillows and eiderdowns.

'I don't want to go!'

Isabel stared at her son, stunned by his vehemence. An anxious lump had formed in her throat. She swallowed and reasoned calmly, 'When your papa told you about Redgrave Park, you seemed eager to go there and invite your friends to stay.'

Marcus looked mutinous still. 'Is Papa going there with us?'

'No. But I expect he will visit us when he is able. You know he has at present some business to attend to with your uncles here in London. He cannot be with us all the time.'

Marcus's face suddenly brightened. 'I shall stay here in London with Papa when you go to the big house in Suffolk.'

'Don't be silly, Marcus!' Isabel chided with a dazed little laugh. 'Of course you must come with me.'

'Robert is staying with his papa while his mama is away. And his Aunt Caroline looks after him and takes him on outings.'

'That is only because his Scottish grandfather is very ill. I'm sure Robert's mother will soon be home to look after him.'

'Aunt June might take me out and look after me.'

'It is not that simple!' Isabel's burst of exasperation was sharpened by hurt. The notion that she might be dispensable to the child who had altered the course of her life had never occurred to her and the shock registered in her wan face. Had she found Marcus his father only to lose him herself?

'I'm afraid you must do as you are told, Marcus. *We* are going to Suffolk.'

When he remained sullen-faced, she attempted cajolery. 'Do you not want to go fishing and riding the fields with Michael Murphy?'

The lure didn't work. He shook his blond head. 'I might later on, I suppose. But now I want to stay here with Papa.'

'I cannot just *leave* you here,' Isabel cried distressfully. 'Your father will be home soon.

I have sent him a note at his club. We shall see what *he* has to say.'

When Etienne received his wife's brief summons to immediately return home it brought a slow thoughtful smile to his lips. A confrontation between them had been imminent for some time. He had been patiently awaiting it. He had sensed that Isabel was ready to explode the vacuum between them. His dread had been that she might opt to settle for that suffocating civility that was their marriage. Yet, despite her aloofness, he'd noticed she couldn't always conceal her pleasure on discovering he'd slept at home on a particular night. God knows he hated playing at a gaming table into the small hours as an excuse not to go back to be tormented by an unlocked door…that was nevertheless impregnable.

At times over the past months, the maxim that absence makes the heart grow fonder had seemed to him to be profound wisdom. On other occasions leaving her alone to brood on their problems seemed to be rank stupidity. His desire to simply storm in and demand she tell him outright whether she loved or hated him was not easily quashed.

Etienne thus arrived home in the spirit of a man taking heed of the fact that what transpired in the next hour would be critical to his future happiness. When he noticed the packing case in the hall, philosophy was abandoned. A demand to know where was his wife was barked at his butler. He was taking the stairs two at a time before he had properly heard Forbes' reply.

Marcus charged to the door at his father's abrupt appearance and, as usual, imprisoned his muscular thighs in an embrace. A dark hand instinctively cupped his blond head, but Etienne's eyes were on the open trunk digging an indent into the quilt on his wife's bed.

As fierce brown eyes met hers, Isabel's chin went up and she smoothed the skirts of her sturdy twill travelling skirts.

'Are you leaving me?'

'I'm leaving London…yes.' As if to reinforce that statement she picked up her bonnet and smoothed her amber curls in readiness to don it.

'Why?'

'Because…I made a mistake in ever coming here. Because I have had enough of this charade that is our marriage,' she informed him with a quiet dignity that was at odds with the flinging of the bonnet back on to the nightstand.

Simultaneously Etienne and Isabel flicked glances at their watchful son.

Etienne held the door wide and gently propelled Marcus outside.

Before Marcus dashed off, he appealed to his father. 'Might I stay with you, Papa? I don't want to go with Mama to the big house in Suffolk.'

'I'll talk to you later.'

The sound of childish feet pounding the landing boards died away.

Etienne strolled closer to the bed. A casual hand violently rammed the case shut. In an instant it was heaved to the floor, and a foot sent it skidding to the wainscot.

'What have I done wrong? My behaviour has been impeccable. I've stayed out of your bed, paid the bills, arranged for our son's schooling. What else do you want me to do, Isabel? Tell me!'

Isabel faced him across an expanse of pure white sheets that might have been the murkiest territory both were afraid to invade.

The savage pain in his eyes made her heart leap to her throat. 'It is not all your fault,' she offered huskily. 'It was wrong of me to force you to marry me. You knew from the outset that it would not work. You said duty would never be quite enough for either of us, and you were right.' She briefly paused. 'But it might have been tolerable a while longer. I asked…expected you to be discreet. I said that I wanted nothing from you but some of your time and your discretion. You have given me…us…very little of either.' Her eyes flinched from his, for she could feel the betraying hotness in them as she succumbed to the lure of his presence. Even crumpled clothes and a dangerous air of louche virility couldn't detract from the appeal he held for her. Her stomach was brimful of butterflies. It would have been so easy to fall into his arms and beg him to love her.

'When have I not been discreet? When have I refused my company when you asked for it?' he demanded.

Isabel glanced at him and snapped, 'I think you know the answer to that.'

'Are you referring to when I said I was too busy to accompany you and Marcus to the waxworks?'

'Yes, I am. You were too busy to take your son out, yet you found time enough to rush to your mistress's side when she summoned you with a note in the middle of the afternoon.'

Etienne looked at her and frowned.

'Don't deny it,' she cried. 'And don't blame Connor or William for letting it slip out that you didn't go to the boxing match with them.'

'Ah...*that* note.' A sudden glint of amusement fired his eyes.

'Yes, *that* note,' Isabel fumed. 'Which leads me to ask whether you think *that* is discreet behaviour. Or that it is discreet to kiss your paramour when your wife is close by. Or that it is respectful to arrange for that...that woman to patronise your wife in company.' The tears that slipped over her lashes were furiously dashed away. '*That* is why I am leaving.

Marcus tells me he wants to stay with you. I have said he must come with me. I hope you will not even think of indulging him in this.'

'For a while, Isabel, I thought there might be some hope for us. I thought if I let you be you might forgive me, remember what it was that first drew us together. Not the lust,' he said softly, then for the first time felt churlish to have made her blush. 'Something else; that inner sense you had that we were special to each other. But you continue to distrust me, and I can't blame you for that. I need a lifetime to make it up to you, not a few months.

'Yes, I did receive a note from a woman that day. It was from my mother. Claudine is returned from Ireland and distraught because Vincent resisted her demands that he marry her. In the role of scorned woman she's upset him to a degree that he is refusing to pay her bills. I have been settling them and have sent her off to visit my sister in Bath before she bankrupts me. Besides, if she stays in London, she might meddle in our domestic troubles, whilst we are regaled with her woes. I don't want my marriage to be as grim as was my parents,' he told her, his tone heartbreakingly hoarse.

'As for Valerie Avery, I have seen her once since I married you. It was the evening she welcomed you back to London. I knew nothing of her plan to do that. But I admit I was grateful to her for it. Yes, she kissed me—in farewell. We both knew our relationship was finished. But I won't say she wasn't a good friend to me or that I wasn't fond of her. I don't love her. In a way, I wish I could.'

'I don't know whether you're telling the truth.' Isabel's turmoil was plain in her strained face.

Etienne grunted a mirthless laugh. 'I know. That's why I despair of there being any hope for us. That's why I wish I could love Valerie. She said to me at Fairbright's ball that it must be wonderful to love one's spouse. It isn't; it's hell. Loving you, Isabel, and knowing you despise me is torture. A fitting punishment, I suppose, for the way you have suffered because of me. I watched my father die a little each day because my mother wouldn't love him, yet he couldn't crush his feelings for her. I promised myself that I would never allow that to happen to me…'

Isabel stared at him with unblinking green eyes. 'How could you possibly think I despise you?' she whispered. 'If I have made it appear so, then I'm sorry. All I ever wanted was to know you cared.' Then, because her son was inextricably part of her, she blurted, 'Do you love Marcus, too?'

'Yes. But not yet with the strength of feeling I have for you. You're the source. Loving him springs from loving you.' He smiled ruefully. 'It's not a ploy to make you stay with me. It's not blackmail. It's just the way it is.'

Isabel started to speak, moistened her lips. A hand fluttered to her face, covered the beginnings of her joyful tears.

'Don't cry. It doesn't matter. Just stay with me…please. I swear I'll treat you well, and Marcus.'

Isabel's head bowed into two hands.

'Don't make me beg, Isabel.' It was a raw request, no more than a murmur. 'I will if you want. I know you deserve to see me humbled.'

Isabel nodded, snuffled into her palms.

'You want to see me beg? Or is that an agreement to stay with me?' The hint of humour in his tone was belied by the tremor in his voice.

Isabel quickly turned her back, hiding her watery face from him until she could bring some order to her appearance. 'It is both,' eventually emerged in a tear-choked voice. 'You ought to beg—as I did. So many nights I sold my soul to the darkness, hoping to bring you back. I'd look at the stars, know you saw the same ones, and will you to think of me. I wept at the thought you might again be a prisoner and prevented from returning, then fantasised you would bravely deem all physical hurt nothing when compared to the agony of our separation. When daylight and reason came, I raged at you, made excuses for you…but I never stopped loving you, Etienne. No one could slander you well enough to make me do that.'

It was Etienne's turn to shield his distress. His head tipped up and he gazed at a splintering ceiling. 'I'm sorry.' It was simply said, but the two words were entreating her not to have him grovelling on his knees. 'Do you love me

now, Isabel?' It was a faltering, almost diffi-
dent, pleading.

Fair curls were shaken away from damp
cheeks. Tear-spiky clumps of lashes parted,
showing him glowing green eyes that promised
him his dignity.

He looked at her, then blinked away the
moisture filming his vision. 'You do,' he muttered with some astonishment.

'Yes, I do,' she told him in a voice husky
with reassurance. 'Of course I do. I knew
you'd come back for Marcus and me...
someday.'

He coughed, sniffed, took stock. 'Will you
come to bed with me?' he gauchely blurted
out.

She nodded.

Etienne swiped a hand over his mouth, his
eyes devouring her over the top of it. 'Are you
sure?'

'Yes.'

She noticed his dark fingers jump, then hes-
itate before fumbling at his neckcloth. In a moment it was off and the front of his shirt was
gaping to reveal a column of strong brown
throat.

'Etienne! You can't mean now,' Isabel gasped out. 'It is...it is after noon. Marcus might come back...or the servants arrive to clean.'

In a moment he had locked the door and his jacket was flung towards a chair. Then he was walking slowly towards her. The large hands framing her radiant, grubby face were trembling. 'Don't say no. Not now. Forbes will keep them all away. I swear to be quiet, and you must try to be too...not like last time...'

The serious desperation in his voice made her giggle and bury her face against his shoulder. 'There are some things about that time I see you have not forgotten.'

'I've lived them over and over in my mind a thousand times since you reminded me of them,' he said huskily and soothed her blushing with a stroking hand.

'You didn't really forget me at all...did you?'

'No,' he vowed softly and felt quietly astonished as a treasury in his mind finally surrendered its soulful secret. Isabel accepted the truth, and, for the first time in eight years, her arms wound about his neck. A seductive peep up at him from beneath long lashes preceded, 'I hope you have not forgot what it was we did…for I liked it very much.'

He smiled against her soft, parted mouth and a voice of gravelly velvet reassured her. 'I haven't, sweet, don't worry about that.'

'Good, for we've no time for a rehearsal,' was all she cheekily said, then was kissing him with such innocent ardour, such sweet longing, that she wasn't even aware when they found the bed.

'Marcus wants a brother. He told me so.'

Isabel dreamily, caressingly, shifted her face on her husband's warm chest. 'And what did you say to that?'

'I said I would see what I could do.'

Isabel raised herself on an elbow. Sated and blissful, she traced his jaw with a languid finger. 'I've told you not to promise him things he might not have.'

Etienne drew her head down to his, kissed her with wooing tenderness. 'I've never promised him a single thing he can't have, Isabel,' he said softly. 'But you'll have to help me in this…for Marcus's sake…'

Epilogue

'Sit by me.' The boy patted the stair by his hip. Automatically one of his arms fell fondly about the infant who curved trustingly against him.

'Mama might be cross if she catches me. But if you are hungry, I'll get you something,' he bravely promised.

The child nodded its curly flaxen head against his arm. A thumb found a dewy mouth and large green eyes looked up through the dusk, glossy and alert.

'Do you want just biscuits or some of Cook's cinnamon bread, too?'

'Drink.'

'And a drink,' the boy echoed with a nod. 'We shall have a midnight feast,' he decided, smiling into the adoring eyes fixed on his face.

Suddenly a door below opened and a gentleman and lady came out followed by the children's parents. The boy watched them walk, quietly conversing, from the dining room to the drawing room. On the threshold of the drawing room his mother and father hesitated, drew back, then kissed before following their guests into the room.

'Wait here.'

Within a moment the boy was back with a cinnamon-fragrant cloth made into a sack and a cup that held milk.

'Come on.' He held out a hand. The girl immediately extracted a wet thumb from her mouth and placed damp fingers in her brother's.

With a sigh of utter contentment Marcus Forrester Hauke led his sister back to bed.

*   *   *   *   *